Rose Ann,

I have many fond memories of you. Lets get together in Florida.

Enjoy!

Jim & Gail

(518) 429-3795

A Lonely Battle Stance

JAMES J. CONNELL, JR.

9/26/15

Copyright © 2014 James J. Connell, Jr.

All rights reserved. No part of this book may be reproduced, stored, or transmitted by any means—whether auditory, graphic, mechanical, or electronic—without written permission of both publisher and author, except in the case of brief excerpts used in critical articles and reviews. Unauthorized reproduction of any part of this work is illegal and is punishable by law.

ISBN: 978-1-4834-2041-7 (sc)
ISBN: 978-1-4834-2040-0 (hc)
ISBN: 978-1-4834-2042-4 (e)

Because of the dynamic nature of the Internet, any web addresses or links contained in this book may have changed since publication and may no longer be valid. The views expressed in this work are solely those of the author and do not necessarily reflect the views of the publisher, and the publisher hereby disclaims any responsibility for them.

Any people depicted in stock imagery provided by Thinkstock are models, and such images are being used for illustrative purposes only. Certain stock imagery © Thinkstock.

Lulu Publishing Services rev. date: 12/01/2014

CONTENTS

Editor's note: Talk about ironies. When I first started writing this book about 10 years ago one of my characters was the daughter of a runaway slave. She learned to read and write as a child, even though southern laws of the time prohibited educating negro slaves. When she was freed after the Civil War she became a teacher of young negro children herself.

The irony is, that at the time, I was not at all familiar with LuLu Publishing, yet the name that I just happened to select for this character was – LuLu.

I thought about changing her name just so it doesn't look "cheesy" but instead I opted to add this coincidence.

He answered President Abraham Lincoln's first call to join the union army in 1861 and keep the country from being torn in half, yet he would not see conventional battle until four years later.

> *Where was he?*
>
> *Would he stand his ground?*

Heinrich Thibaut was a Civil War soldier who was forced beyond the conventional battlefield directly into a situation that was as violent and intense, yet much more personal. He questions the meaning of the war and his role in it. He suffers disabling injuries, escapes from a deadly Confederate prison camp, gets a close-up look at slavery and then the horrific, blood-drenched killing fields of Gettysburg. Then, in the midst of it all – he meets the young female love of his life. He is torn, but the enemy is still threatening.

FOREWORD

Heinrich Thibaut responded to President Abraham Lincoln's initial call for 75,000 volunteers in 1861 to help suppress the rebel insurrection, yet not fire a shot directly at the enemy for nearly four years.

He was not a coward, a deserter, or a bounty jumper, but he was about as far from wanting to be a dead hero as any 20-year-old could be.

He will have opportunities to join fighting infantry units from his hometown of Erie, Pennsylvania, and confront the Confederate enemy.

He'll question: Is the American Civil War about freeing slaves, saving the union, or states rights to self-determination? Is it, as it came to be called by some, "A rich man's war, but a poor man's fight."

Does he ultimately "see the elephant" (hold his ground in the face of enemy fire) when his country needs him the most?

As was the case with nearly every other American during this chilling period, the Civil War will drag him in, challenge him, test his convictions and change his life and the lives of his future generations forever.

Mid-way through the war, he re-enlisted in his second unit for a $25 bounty in Cleveland, Ohio, but he ends up in Troy, New York, where, during the height of the war, while death and destruction abound nationwide, he meets the love of his life (whom he will ultimately marry). But, she is forbidden love, because he is not where he belongs - off to war!

Where is the heroism here? What is there to respect? Thibaut was among the first to volunteer and does serve his time honorably as a soldier, but only after he makes a personal stand. Instead of following the masses blindly to their graves, he asks, for what purpose are we making this sacrifice? In Civil War times, that makes him unique and odd, though to some, a hero in a sense.

ACKNOWLEDGEMENTS

This book is dedicated to my sister Debbie who was the first person many years ago to encourage me to write. She also helped me to get my first newspaper reporter's job. Thanks Deb!

Also dedicated to my loyal wife, Gail, who not only edited it over and over again, but "cleaned it up" the same as she has been doing with all the other stuff I've "dumped on her" over the course of more than 40 years.

Final dedication: To my granddaughter Karlina Marie Connell and my 11 other grandkids. By allowing me to share my Civil War enthusiasm with them they have assured my passion will live on.

"War is at best barbarism…its glory is all moonshine. It is only those who have neither fired a shot, nor heard the shrieks and groans of wounded who cry aloud for more blood, more vengeance, more desolation…War is Hell."
Union Gen. William Tecumseh Sherman

CHAPTER 1

WE ARE COMING ABRAHAM

In 1859, as tensions between the North and South mounted, Erie County sheriff and longtime business owner, John W. McLane formed the Wayne Guards militia company in Erie, Pennsylvania.

When President Abraham Lincoln made his very first call in 1861 for northern volunteer soldiers to help protect the union 19-year-old, Heinrich Thibaut was among the first to join McLane's Erie Regiment.

At 5' 9" tall, the strapping, gray-eyed, lifelong, Erie resident, was typical of those Lincoln had in mind when he asked for volunteers willing to help suppress the rebellion that became the American Civil War.

In those times, no city could be considered more typically northern than Erie. If Atlanta, Georgia was to be considered the heart of Dixie, then Erie certainly could have been a prime candidate for the same honor in Yankee territory.

By the time the American Civil War was over, nearly half of the eligible Erie County men (about 5,000) served their country honorably; Heinrich Thibaut is one who did - he didn't just rush into it blindly though, the way most did.

Forecasting civil war in 1859, abolitionist zealot, John Brown led 16 white men and five negro men to the federal armory at the confluence of the Shenandoah and Potomac Rivers in, what is now, Harper's Ferry, W. Virginia.

"One man and God can overturn the universe," Brown declared, as he revealed his plan to use spears and pikes that he had designed and guns that he would steal from the arsenal to arm slaves of the south into a massive rebellion against their oppressors.

Brown counted on two of his black "soldiers" to rouse thousands of slaves to "swarm." to the cause - None came.

Instead, Lieutenant Colonel Robert E. Lee, U.S. Army, and his former West Point student Lt. James Ewell Brown (JEB) Stuart arrived with a company of Marines, (Both of whom ultimately would become great confederate generals). The resulting three-minute clash would lead to casualties for many of Brown's followers, including two of his own sons.

Brown and his surviving followers were charged with treason, conspiracy to forment servile insurrection, and murder from this and previous incidents. They were hung at Charlestown, Virginia on December 2, 1859, and were immediately proclaimed martyrs by Northern abolitionists.

Much to the embarrassment of the Virginia government, Brown did not die like a crazed fanatic. He sat atop his coffin as they carried him to the gallows encouraging the crowd to cheer and celebrate his martyrdom. At his sentencing, he made this grim prognostication of things to come that would consume the country for most of the upcoming decade.

"Now, if it is deemed necessary that I should forfeit my life for the furtherance of the ends of justice, and mingle my blood further with the blood of my children and with the blood of millions in this slave country whose rights are disregarded by the wicked, cruel, and unjust enactments - I submit; so let it be done," Brown said. "...the crimes of this guilty land will never be purged away but with blood..."

John McLane was very much aware of the growing hostility within the nation and, was in the majority when he predicted, war between the states after he returned from President Lincoln's Inaugural Address in early 1861.

When these premonitions came true and the Confederates fired upon Fort Sumter, South Carolina on April 12,1861, Lincoln made his call for 75,000 volunteers to restore the union.

McLane was the first man from northwestern Pennsylvania in the field making his own call for volunteers. Having served as Captain of the Wayne Guards (naming it in honor of General "Mad" Anthony Wayne) during the War with Mexico some twenty years prior, that "old war-horse," John McLane was commissioned Colonel of his re-born militia by proclamation of the Pennsylvania governor on April 21, 1861.

In only four days 1,200 men responded to McLane's call. They came from the hills of Erie, Crawford and Wayne, into the city of Erie.

Heinrich Thibaut, and his older brother, Conrad, were among the first men in the nation to volunteer to help suppress the rebel insurrection.

A spot of ground for a camp was soon selected in the eastern part of town and called Camp Wayne. There was hurrying to and fro in preparation for war. Tents were procured, sheds and cook houses were constructed. Area farmers came pouring in with wagon loads of provisions for the country's gallant defenders.

In camp, Thibaut and the other men would learn the rudiments in the rugged and arduous duties of basic soldiering. Including everything from dress parades to how to live upon hard fare and to sleep on the cold ground.

Patriotic women turned out to ensure the men were properly uniformed before departing for the seat of war. Needles and sewing machines were kept busy night and day creating a handsome uniform consisting of a blue jacket and pants, and a shirt of yellow flannel. This suit was a compromise between the Zouave (a colorful French-inspired combination predominately of red and blue, used by many units throughout the war) and the conventional federal uniform of a four-button, dark blue sack coat and light blue trousers, both made of wool.

McLane's Erie Regiment, as they would affectionately come to be known, donned one of the most singular and picturesque uniforms seen during the entire four years of the American Civil War.

Long-time businessman and Erie resident, Strong Vincent, who ultimately played such a glorious part in the history of his famous Eighty-Third Pennsylvania Volunteer Infantry, until his death at Gettysburg in 1863, was designated adjutant of the regiment by McLane.

On Arpil 29, in the midst of a drenching rain, the regimental band led them up State Street to the train depot and on to rail cars for Pittsburgh. The roar of artillery salutes mingled with the tears and waving handkerchiefs as they departed.

As the first regiment to enter Pittsburgh, they were received with even more pomp and circumstance, and pride of going to glorious war.

They settled in Camp Wilkins, which quickly became the rendezvous for all volunteers from western Pennsylvania. McLane was appointed commander of the camp.

Guard mounts were established and military order and discipline included regular company and regimental-sized drill, which would attract thousands of civilian spectators. Battalion drill always wound up with a dress parade and the Erie Regiment was the only uniformed and organized regiment, which also included its own band at that point.

They remained at Camp Wilkins for six weeks until it became overcrowded. A new camp (Camp Wright) was laid out twelve miles up the Allegheny River along a pleasant hill which sloped gradually to the river's edge. Surrounded by high ranges and mountains, which threw a cool and refreshing shade over the camp, the men bathed in the river, ate well and calmly sported away the hours while waiting a call to war.

They rambled over a future career of glory, and of a war that many felt would only last weeks or months, little realizing that for most of them the perils, horrors and hardships of war lay ahead.

CHAPTER 2

WHERE TO GO FROM CAMP WRIGHT?

For Heinrich Thibaut and about six hundred other men those horrors would not be as soon in coming, nor, as intense as for the majority. The general feeling throughout the north and the south was that the war would be short-lived, and their cause was the just one, with the same God on their side. Both exuded confidence of rapid military victory for themselves. Therefore, many of the early volunteers only enlisted for three months of military service. This applied to many of the members of the Erie Regiment, including the Thibaut brothers.

In the beginning, there was more of a feeling in the north that their purpose was to suppress a rebel insurrection, acting more as policemen, rather than going to actual war against a Confederate nation with armies of thousands at a time.

Few people on either side seemed to realize, or admit, they were in for actual war in which masses would suffer and die, including women and children. Northerners would slowly come to realize that it was going to take a major commitment of lives and a number of years to destroy a valiant, well-lead, zealous rebel army that felt their country was being invaded, one which was willing to fight to the death to create an independent nation.

Most of the Erie Regiment members eventually enlisted in the 83rd, 111th or the 145th Pennsylvania, Infantry Regiments after their three month obligation, or shortly afterward. These units were among the most glorified and active in almost every major engagement of the war. Including the suicidal-full-frontal assault of Marye's Heights at Fredericksburg along with the heroic defense of the southern slope of Little Round Top at Gettysburg.

The Thibauts did not join those regiments.

But for those three months prior to the Civil War, most of which were spent in the pleasantries of what would be named Camp Wright, life was so casual that in latter years of the war many veterans of those Pennsylvania units would look back during the midst of some perilous campaign in the wilds of Virginia and cast a longing glance back to those tranquil and happy times.

At Camp Wright the regiment was supplied with muskets, this infused new life into the men since they could finally take target practice.

At least two or three times they would get actual marching orders to prepare to go into battle. On one occasion, everything was packed up and readied for movement in the direction of the enemy, but orders were rescinded within twenty-four hours.

Now, two months had passed since Heinrich and the others had first answered the call, leaving him with the feeling that they would never be called to battle. This had a negative effect on the morale and discipline for some of the men. They had come out to fight, not to play summer soldier. They began to criticize the state government and freely question its partiality. They had not been paid and never mustered into the service of the United States.

It was when the soldier's morale was lowest that something strange happened that would add a romantic and inventive turn in camp. Heinrich and some of his buddies were walking along the shore one day when they spotted a clam shell imbedded beneath the crystal tide. It was glistening in all the glory of its pearly incandescence. The idea came about to fashion a ring out of the shell for a loved one at home. Using available tools including a file, jack-knife, bayonet and sandstone a jewel was turned out the next day. The news of the great discovery spread throughout the camp from company to company and regiment to regiment with great adulation for the inventor. There was a simultaneous rush to the river in search of clam shells and other items to be transformed.

For the next three weeks there was a concentrated buzz of the instruments as men stole away from drill, roll-call and dress parade to go fashion rings and jewels of beauty. Men even feigned illness to find time away from guard duty, or they carried their clam-shells along with them. Soon the "ring factory" took priority over going off to battle and the lack of a payday. The camp became a grand bazaar for their sale and purchase, not only to other soldiers but visiting civilians. The greater the demand, the greater the manufacture.

It was in this peaceful valley during the three months of service that these men came together while plying the occupation of a soldier. This was of great benefit when it came to organize, drill, live, fight, and for many, to ultimately die together.

It was written and said that as a regiment, the Erie boys would have fought bravely; being all active and vigorous young men who were among the very first to volunteer. But their three months expired, so paymaster Veech came around and paid the regiment for one month and 17 days. It was mid-July 1861 and they were discharged to their homes with war still pending. However, the options to participate and on what level were left up to each individual. It was common knowledge throughout the military and civilian communities a battle between the armies was within days, especially since Lincoln was pressing Gen. George McClellan, commander of the Union, to finally attack the rebel army which was camped across the Potomac River and a constant threat to Washington, D.C.

Of never having been called to face the foe in a single battle, Pennsylvania Private O.W. Norton wrote on July 14, 1861:

> "The Erie regiment is one grand fizzle out. We left home full of fight, earnestly desiring a chance to mingle with the hosts under the Stars and Stripes. For two months we drilled steadily, patiently waiting the expected orders which never came, but to be countermanded. We have now come to the conclusion that we will have no chance, and we are waiting in sullen silence and impatience for the expiration of our time."

Many Erie Regiment soldiers, including Heinrich and his brother barely reached home, when on July 21, the news of the great Union debacle at Bull Run (Manassas, Va.) aroused the nation to a new sense of danger. This opened their eyes to the fact that they were in for a prolonged bloody war.

The American Civil War had begun!!!

The first major engagement of the Civil War began after Union commander Brig. Gen. Irwin McDowell and his equivalent confederate counterparts, Albert Sidney Johnston and Pierre Gustave Toutant (P.G.T.) Beauregard took a few days to properly position their troops for battle.

Both sides exuded confidence that they would emerge victorious after this one grand battle that could end the war. They felt it would be little more than a wrestling match with bullets flying.

Several U.S. congressmen, other dignitaries and their ladies wheeled their carriages from Washington just a few miles south to Centreville. Many brought blankets and picnic baskets thinking it would be just another unique way to spend a Sunday afternoon.

Both armies began by trying to turn the other's flank, leaving the Union at an advantage. Gen. Thomas Jackson's rebels secured a position at the crest of a hill and held the point. Brig. Gen. Bernard

Bee rallied his own men and shouted, "There is Jackson standing like a stone wall," hence the name "Stonewall Jackson." Bee was immediately killed by an enemy bullet. Jackson's hard defense of that hill turned the day. The Union retreat became a bloody rout as soldiers crashed past frightened civilians who also had to scatter for their lives.

In less than one day, fleeing Union troops covered as much ground as it had taken them two and a half days to cover on the way to Bull Run. Out of 18,752 Federal infantry and artillerymen, 460 were dead, 1,124 were wounded and 1,312 were missing. Confederate numbers are out of 18,053, infantry, cavalry and artillerymen, 387 were dead, 1,582 wounded, 13 missing.

Despite similar numbers, it was obviously a decisive rebel victory and the morale booster they had hoped for. Southern states had now seceded, declared their independence from federal rule and domination, and proved they would fight to the death to maintain their "freedom."

For the North, Bull Run satisfied the craving for action but disappointed their expectations of bringing the war to a quick and victorious conclusion. The defeat was dispiriting. After the initial shock had passed, soldiers seized the opportunity with stubborn determination to save the Union or die trying.

CHAPTER 3

THE FAMOUS 83ᴿᴰ IS BORN

By July 24, Col. John McLane received an order from the Hon. Simon Cameron, Secretary of War, issuing a call to reorganize the Erie boys. In five weeks, nearly a thousand responded, including about three hundred from the discharged Erie Regiment, who formed the nucleus for a new, destined-to-be famous, Pennsylvania regiment.

On September 8th they were mustered in to service in the United States Army for three years, assigned to the Third Brigade in the Army of the Potomac (the main fighting federal body of the war.) and the famous 83rd Pennsylvania Infantry Regiment was born.

The Thibaut boys still did not respond while other former members of the Erie Regiment rushed to join the 83rd, 111th and 145th Infantry Regiments, and other Pennsylvania units. There were Erie boys involved in almost every major battle and event of the war from beginning to the end.

Involvement was almost immediate for the 83rd as the Army of the Potomac moved onto the Virginia Peninsula. By 1862 the 83rd had obtained the reputation as one of the best regiments in the army, having fought at Gaines Mills, Malvern Hill, Second Manassas and Antietam.

The real test for the 83rd was at the Battle of Gaines Mills on June 27, 1862. McLane and his men were east of Richmond along the wooded banks of Boatswain Swamp preparing a defense against the Confederates who were aimed at the newly formed Fifth Army Corps. The 83rd was in a brigade that was isolated from the rest of the army. Brig. Gen. Daniel Butterfield sent an order to McLane to defend his position stubbornly.

McLane responded, "Tell Gen. Butterfield he needn't have sent me such orders, I intend to hold it." The first assault came as Confederate Gen. James Longstreet was repelled by the Union line.

McLane turned to his men and said the battle is far from over, "You'll see enough of them before night, boys." The 83rd and Butterfield's brigade would repel two more assaults, before their flank was exposed by a successful charge of Gen. John Hood's Texans.

McLane, immediately realizing the seriousness of the situation, ordered the regiment to change its front to face the new threat. While conducting this movement, the 83rd was fired upon again. Suddenly, McLane was slammed by bullets to the head and chest as his lifeless body plummeted to the ground. Within minutes, other senior officers and men became casualties. The 83rd managed to rally around the colors and hold against three more assaults until they were eventually forced to withdraw.

The bravery and persistence displayed by McLane and the 83rd at the Battle of Gaines Mills remains a lasting tribute. McLane instilled the sense of discipline and created the fighting character in his early Erie Regiment men and passed the same to their descendents, in the 83rd. The 83rd would go on to fight in numerous battles, including Gettysburg and the Wilderness. Gaines Mills was their "trial-by-fire."

With McLane's death, Strong Vincent succeeded to the Colonelcy of the 83rd after a battle with malaria, which left him bedridden during Gaines Mills, Malvern Hill, Second Manassas and Antietam.

At Fredericksburg in December, 1862, Vincent debuted and won the admiration and confidence of his men and officers when his brigade was pinned down by victorious Confederate fire. He rose to his feet, sword in hand and led them to safety under the cover of a passing cloud that blocked the moonlight. He would enhance that reputation of leadership at Chancellorsville.

Vincent and the 83rd helped to save the day on the second of the three days battle of Gettysburg on July 2, 1863, when they rushed to protect Little Round Top just time and set up the famous bayonet defense of the 20th Maine, but the heroic stand would cost Vincent his life.

As both armies moved north into Pennsylvania, this Erie resident foretold his own fate when he informed another staff officer, "What more glorious death can one man desire, than to die in the soil of old Pennsylvania fighting for the flag." At Gettysburg, during the early morning of July 2 while waiting orders, Vincent prophetically commented, "To-day will either bring me my stars, (promotion to general) or finish my career as a soldier."

At about 4 p.m. the Confederate attack of Longstreet began to expose the flank of the Union Third Corps. Within minutes a staff officer approached asking for support for Little Round Top, a key position that was in danger of being taken. Vincent did not wait orders from his division commander, knowing the urgency of the situation. Vincent was the person who positioned Col. Joshua Lawrence Chamberlain and his 20th Maine to ultimately make his famous, desperate bayonet charge down Little Round Top. Vincent's quick thinking and positioning had as much to do with saving the day and the Battle of Gettysburg for the Union as anyone, but he would not live to tell about it.

Vincent was mortally struck in the thigh and the bullet passed through his groin and into his intestines. "This is the fourth time they have shot at me, they have got me at last." Four days later Vincent died from the wound but not before being promoted to Brigadier General.

The 83rd would fight on to glory suffering the second highest number of battle deaths of all Civil War Union regiments. Vincent's old Third Brigade, including the 83rd, was there to receive the Confederate surrender at Appomattox on April 9, 1865.

The 111th, the second regiment from the counties of Northwest Pennsylvania fought in both theaters of the war from Antietam to Gettysburg in the east, to the west at Lookout Mountain and Durham Station. The 111th was the first regiment to enter Atlanta, raising its colors atop City Hall and was with Gen. William T. Sherman during his march to sea in 1864.

The 145th was at Fredericksburg, Chancellorsville, Gettysburg, Grant's Overland Campaign, the Siege of Petersburg and Appomattox.

Heinrich Thibaut received news of the heroism, the victories, the defeats and the tragic deaths of his friends and leaders the same as most civilians did, through newspaper accounts and word of mouth. He was not present to witness or participate in the events.

CHAPTER 4

WHAT ARE WE FIGHTING FOR?

Col. Strong Vincent was buried in Erie Cemetery, the same Pennsylvania cemetery that Heinrich would ultimately be buried in. But why didn't Heinrich serve with the 83rd and risk his life on Little Round Top also?

Heinrich Thibaut was no coward. He was not afraid of being a soldier, serving, sacrificing and if necessary dying for the country he loved so much. He just needed his questions answered before making such a commitment.

His parents Phillip Thibaut and Caroline (Hornung) Thibaut settled in Erie in 1833 to raise their family after leaving their native Germany. Phillip was a hard-driving laborer who took a lot of pride in his new country.

Devotion to the Union was strong among immigrant groups such as the Germans who had seen the unhappy effects of division in their native lands and felt a special responsibility for preventing a similar fate from overtaking their adopted country. The union was associated with the ideals and opportunities that helped carry them to America in the first place.

More than three-quarters of the 1,556,000 soldiers in the Union Army, and the approximately 850,000 Confederates, who served during the war were American born.

Germans were the most numerous of foreign-born Yankees. The Northern states in 1860 contained more than a million people who were born in Germany, with the total number of German-born soldiers exceeding 200,000. The Irish were second with nearly 150,000.

Several divisions were made up mostly of Germans. Their technical aptitude was particularly useful in artillery, engineer and signal units. Among foreign soldiers they were also noted for their musical ability and accomplishments, with their favorite song being the stirring "Morgenroth." German troops often sang this in their native tongue while on the march or in camp. Their bands were also among the best in the Army.

Few cities were more typically German than Erie, a growing city, prosperous with new factories, Lake Erie shipping and fishing. Soldiers came from the city and from the many farms and small towns surrounding it.

But before he made a commitment to the Civil War Heinrich Thibaut had many questions he had to answer for himself. In Civil War times he was considered unusual, however in our modern times he could be considered a realist and possibly applauded by some for his courage to resist, rather than blindly following the masses.

The population of the Northern states in 1860, the year before the war began, was 22 million, including four million men of combat age. The Confederate states had a population of about nine million (four million of whom were slaves) including 1,140,000 men of combat age. The 1,117,703 ultimate casualties (including deaths, wounded, desertions and missing in action) on both sides represented 3.6 percent of the total population of the country. About 21 percent - more than one-fifth - of the nation's young men were killed or wounded between 1861 and 1865.

As Henrich explained to his family and friends shortly after Bull Run, he served during those three months, hoping, as did most, that they would be called to face the enemy in one massive battle that would end the entire conflict. Unfortunately, that opportunity would never come for the Erie Regiment.

"Here I just get home and we are met with the shock of the Bull Run confederate victory within days. Hundreds of people died in a battle that was supposed to end this mutiny against our government, but all it has done is prolong it. Now it could go on for years before those damned secessionists bastards give up," Heinrich told his father during the summer of 1861.

"Why are we fighting anyway," he questioned family and friends. Which is the main question that has been asked innumerable times throughout history.

To this day there is no clear-cut answer.

Many southerners, and even some northerners will say the American Civil was about state's rights, with the Confederates seeking "freedom" from the centralized Federal Government.

Other people will give the quick, simple answer that the Civil War was fought to free slaves.

The truth is, they are both are abstractly correct in a sense, because had slavery not existed, the Civil War never would have happened.

There is no simple, or single, clear-cut cause for the war as it was a very complex series of economic, social and political differences and issues. But as a result, African-Americans who were held in bondage in Southern states were set free. But even that was not accomplished without much debate and questioning among those in charge in the Federal Government, including Lincoln himself.

At the core of Southern right's to self-determination was the hottest issue of the times - slavery. The North was not so much opposed to slavery as it existed, but wanted to keep it from spreading in to new territories west of the Mississippi River, including Kansas and Nebraska.

Lincoln was not shy about saying his priority was saving the Union. If he could accomplish that without freeing a single slave, he said he would have. If saving the Union meant freeing every slave, he would gladly do that, he added.

But the average citizen/soldier, especially in the south, was too busy trying to survive and prosper in their own lives rather than burden themselves with complex issues that would lead them to four years of the ugliest fighting in American history.

Prior to the Civil War, people identified more with their individual states rather than one centralized federal government. In some cases, particularly in the south, respective states were considered self-sufficient countries by their population. The country was more commonly referred to as America. It wasn't until after the war, that the term and concept of the United States of America really emerged.

Thibaut was typical of many soldiers and civilians in the North based on an opinion he expressed in early 1862.

"I know little about slavery, but what I have seen, they don't seem all that unhappy, always singin', dancin' and playin', he said. "We're not fightin' to free slaves, but to put down the rebellion and save the union. Let's worry about winning the war then we can fret about free'in the damned darkies that their all complainin' over."

As harsh as his opinions might seem today, many Northerners agreed, especially as the war dragged on. There were strong concerns that if the concentration was on abolishing slavery the conflict would be prolonged at a greater cost of lives and money.

There were also feelings that African-Americans were ignorant and irresponsible, and that they would come north to compete for jobs with a great sympathy on their side. This was a particular concern among immigrant groups such as the Irish and Germans.

"I do not intend to shirk as long there is something worth fightin' for...I mean freedom," Heinrich added.

Heinrich had a history of being misunderstood. Today, he would be labeled a maverick or a loner. Much of his time growing up was spent on hobbies, including molding and performing as a circus tumbler, a talent that had been passed to many German children.

While he was a grade school student he worked as an apprentice for the owner of an area molding operation, who taught him the trade. The shop owner allowed Heinrich to take the small scrap pieces home rather than discard them. He molded these into various practical and ornamental forms. His favorite things to create were Revolutionary War and Mexican War figures and massive displays, small weapons and bullets. He also fashioned many rings, jewelry and household items.

When Heinrich was about 12-years-old the family home was facing foreclosure after his father sustained a knee injury that left him laid up for most of a year. Heinrich gathered all of the items he had created to that point and presented them to his parents to sell. The family was surprised to find that he had hundreds of items that showed great skill in creating and imagination. Not only did they make enough money to save the home, but Heinrich and family set up a small business selling things that he created on an ongoing basis.

Heinrich was a below-average school student. His teachers blamed it on daydreaming, because his mind seemed to always be on his next metal creation or circus performance. He had a ninth-grade education.

His fascination with the circus stemmed from family roots. He had a number of aunts and uncles who were associated with the circus in one form or the other. That fascination became enhanced each time the circus passed through Erie to the point of where he ran away with the circus as a teen but returned just before the war.

According to an application that Heinrich's wife filed in 1898, while seeking a military widow's pension, she wrote, "when as a youth about 16 to 17 years of age he left home and while gone joined a circus company."

Heinrich would finally leave his parent's home for good in 1862. He left to join the circus again, but would end up in the middle of the tragic Civil War.

CHAPTER 5

NEAR DEATH IN MURFREESBORO

The circus slowly made it's way to Cleveland, Ohio, with Heinrich as one of it's most talented and popular tumblers. Despite the fact that the country was very much gripped by the war in 1862, circus performances were one the few very popular diversions that average people could afford to enjoy at the time.

Later in life, Heinrich would reflect on this time as being among his happiest memories. One of his roommates was an orphaned boy named Henry Lyons. Lyons' parents were killed while he was in grade school so he became involved with the circus as a young child. They learned more about tumbling from each other and became quick friends. Even in a strange, new, large city such as Cleveland the buzz was still about war and there was still pressure on military-aged men to join, or produce a logical explanation as to why not. This did not leave Heinrich much time to think about his choices.

His immediate future would be decided though on a winter night in 1862, when Lyons came blasting in to their room carrying a recruiting. He announced there was a gathering in city square and new recruits could enlist and immediately be processed and readied for war. There was a bounty (a contemporary term for a bonus for enlistment) of $25 to enlist, he said. The Federal Government offered another $100 in discharge bonuses by then, $25 of which was paid up front, in addition to the first month's pay. A typical Union private earned about $13 a month in salary during the war.

Individual volunteers often enlisted at these recruiting rendezvous more to show their masculinity to the ladies and their peers, rather than any deep-seated belief in the cause. After enlisting, they then took very rudimentary physical, mental and medical tests. They were proudly paraded about as patriotic music blared, ladies cheered, presented gifts and made promises to the new soldiers. Local politicians made grand speeches about courage, glory and victory, and area businessmen often pledged additional bonus incentives to each enlistee. All this happened with little thought to the likelihood their boys could quickly be reduced to nothing more than cannon-fodder from enemy fire.

The concern Heinrich had was experiencing the war, seeing its results early-on, and still trying to remain in a position of being able to choose where he belonged in reference to it.

All the excitement and the sound of one of the most popular songs of the day, *Battle Cry of Freedom*, was just too much for him, an emotional, Heinrich said. He was swept by the excitement at a rally and seeing others enlistees cheered as heroes when they signed up. Swelled with confidence and patriotism, on Jan. 15 1863, twenty-one-year-old, Heinrich Thibaut and Henry Lyons put the circus behind them forever and enlisted for three years as privates at Camp Cleveland and were assigned to Company E of the 10th Regimental Ohio Calvary, commanded by Maj. Gen. William S. Rosencrans.

Heinrich was paid $25 when he enlisted and was due $75 at the end of a three-year enlistment. The 10th was originally part of the Army of the Ohio, but by 1863 it was renamed XVI Corps and later the Army of the Cumberland.

"After signing our names to the roll, we were ordered to report at the old church in center of town, for drill the next morning," Thibaut wrote to his family.

"We were on hand early and found several others already there. After a full day of drilling we realized we had no homes in the city to go to so mattresses were furnished and there we slept all night."

Upon hearing of his enlistment Heinrich's mother wrote him this letter.

"If it is the will of the Lord, know that this fighting business is not all it is made out to be. Heroes die more rapidly than cowards in battle. I fully expect you to be a hero. Do not shirk on my account for if I must sacrifice my son to save this glorious union then so be it. The only time you've ever been away from me is when you went with the circus. I won't be there to protect you anymore. There are some bad men even in the Union Army who would hurt and rob you. You will only get close to a few and have to look over your shoulder at all times. You will be alone, afraid, cold and hungry nearly all the time. You will regret this decision many times but now that you have made this commitment, stick to it. I've included some socks, a shirt and your favorite maple candies. This is all I can do for now as I still have your brothers and sisters to care for. I will send more as I can."

Heinrich could tell by her shaky handwriting and the stained paper that she was crying the whole time. This warmed him that she cared so, yet made him feel guilty for what might come of her should he be killed. He tucked the letter inside the breast pocket of his new four-button, blue, Yankee sackcoat.

The next morning Thibaut and the others were piled into railway cars, or tramped off down the road, many leaving weeping relatives behind them. They bravely boasted of going off to finally "see the elephant," a period slang for facing the enemy in battle. This was derived from witnessing some major event such as an elephant in P.T. Barnum's circus.

The young men of the 1860s, on both sides, carried into military life a strong set of values, including patriotism, commitment to God duty and family. Most had a purely American-Victorian morality and an almost unanimous dedication to face death long before being shamed or dishonored. These values received reinforcement from home, as they went off to war. But, soldiers were often confused and frustrated as they attempted to apply them in combat, camps, prisons and in hospitals of neglect, suffering and countless deaths.

The Civil War regularly betrayed their values and confidence, leaving many shallow and indifferent because much that they encountered was at odds with what they grew up with. Both union and confederate boys were frustrated in their attempts to fight the war as an expression of their values, leaving them harshly disillusioned.

In battle, Civil War soldiers on both sides often maintained their ranks and continued aggressively not necessarily out of courage and commitment, but out of fear of being labeled a coward. In many cases, entire neighborhoods of eligible boys who spent their childhoods together joined the army together, formed their own companies, fought and died side-by-side. Deserters, especially those who ran during the heat of battle, were often executed in front of troops who were forced to watch. Other deserters were subjected to severe punishments and ridicule by officers and men ranging from having to wear sign reading "deserter" to being tarred and feathered, having their heads publicly shaved and dishonorably discharged on the spot. They were left on their own to battle the elements and work their way home. At home they were accountable to citizens who usually realized what happened.

As Heinrich Thibaut left a second time, for what he thought was going to be battle, him and his buddy, Henry Lyons were typical Yankee soldiers.

The 10th Regiment, Ohio Cavalry was organized at Camp Taylor, Cleveland in October 1862 and left the state for Nashville, Tenn. on February 27, 1863, attached to the 2nd Brigade, 2nd Cavalry Division, Army of the Cumberland. It would go on to have a glorious history including at the Battle of Chickamauga, Sept. 19-20, 1863, Battle of Resaca, May 14-15 and the 10 Ohio Cavalry was with Gen. William T. Sherman during his famous March to Sea in 1864.

But, by the time the regiment reached Murfreesboro, Tennessee, during the winter of 1863, it was another "near-miss" for Heinrich to engage the enemy in formal battle.

The Battle of Stones River (as it was known in the North... Murfreesboro in the South) was part of the Western Theater of Operations on Dec. 31, 1862 to Jan. 2, 1863, taking place in Murfreesboro, Tennessee, about 30 miles south east of Nashville.

At that point, much of the Civil War action was in the middle of Tennessee. There Rosencrans was at the head of the Army of the Cumberland and Gen. Braxton Bragg was commander of the Confederate Army of Tennessee.

"Old Rosy," as his troops called Rosencrans, had been sparring with Bragg since the end of October 1862 without taking much initiative with a full-scale encounter. Finally, in battle at Murfreesboro, Rosencrans was able to cob together a defensive line after his army had absorbed a punishing surprise attack as few days prior. This maneuver was key to his eventual victory at Murfreesboro, as he was able to avoid disaster. But, also key, was that he lost valuable ground in Tennessee to Bragg.

As Bragg fled "Old Rosy" decided at last to slowly move to bottle-up Bragg in that state to prevent any Confederate troops from serving as reinforcements along the Mississippi River all the way down to Vicksburg, Miss. Eventually, Rosencrans' deliberation proved effective, for he maneuvered skillfully in such a way to force Bragg to withdraw south of the Tennessee River by the summer of 1863.

However, when Rosencrans exited Murfreesboro shortly after the battle, The 10th Ohio Cavalry was among the many regiments that he left behind for defensive picket and scout purposes. The 10th Ohio also provided the provost guard.

It was during this occupation that Henry Lyons would lose his life and Heinrich would come within inches of losing his when they were attacked in the middle of the night by Confederate cavalry raiders. This attack would not only form Heinrich's Civil War life and cause him to miss conventional battle for the majority of the war, but it would also lead him down a path just as deadly and demanding, yet much more personal

Bragg and his followers often relied on surprise cavalry raids, on bridges, railroads, supply lines, and unsuspecting federal units. Many confederate and some union officers used this method, including one of the greatest cavalry officers of the entire war, rebel Gen. Nathan Bedford Forrest. Raids were used to demoralize the enemy, boost civilian support and gain supplies. Bragg often made raids, rather than persistent advances and conventional battle in Tennessee and other parts of the south.

Even before the Kentucky and Antietam campaigns during 1862, raiders had already had a decisive influence on operations in the West, while conventional warfare was carried on in the east. Southern guerrillas, with many civilian members, were quite active in middle Tennessee, where they controlled the countryside by intimidating union supporters. They not only attacked troops but burned houses and beat and killed civilians. The offensive superiority of the raid would often overcome manpower disadvantages and affect troop movements. When successful, raids on troops would send the adversary fleeing, rather than resisting. The aggressor would then either take over the desired property and personnel or just swoop through, making a quick exit.

A sudden cavalry raid was Heinrich's first exposure to the rebel enemy.

One night he and Lyons were assigned picket duty. Heinrich suddenly heard something like the screeching of bees whip past his head and slam into a soldier a few yards behind him. Heinrich quickly realized that it was actually a confederate 58 cal. Minie' ball, fired from a Springfield rifle. He and Lyons sprung to their feet, screamed "Johnnies," to alert others and reached for their pistols. Heinrich rapidly fired two shots into the darkened woods in the direction where the shot came from and looked toward Lyons. As he turned, Heinrich was blasted with the sounds of bones crushing and a wave of blood that enveloped him. He grabbed for his already-lifeless friend, Henry Lyons, as his body hit the ground. Suddenly, he felt a heavy slam against the back of his neck and everything went black.

The next thing Heinrich experienced was one of the ugliest pictures of war anyone could imagine, he said, later in life.

He was shocked into consciousness by a sudden pain in his right foot caused by a wild swine gnawing at it. In the early morning light he could see other swine groping at skulls and remains of the many dead that lay around him. "I can never forget the impression those wide open eyes made on me. The faces of the dead were horrible and blackened. The pigs rolled skulls and various human parts around in their demonic fest...this is what it's like to die for one's country?," Heinrich questioned.

Heinrich raised his pistol to fire at the pigs when an even more ghastly sound shocked his attention. Only a few feet away, he could hear the sounds of confederates plunging their deadly bayonets in to the bodies of wounded Yankee soldiers. He knew his turn was coming and quickly tried to think of what options he had. As he pushed a small bush aside to get a better view he could see, twinkling in the morning light, the bright gold on a dead union major's shoulder strap. He figured if he could slip that jacket on he might have half a chance of being taken prisoner as an officer, rather than just butchered as a hapless private. He slid the jacket on just in time to reassume the position he had been laying in. His first hope was that the enemy would assume he was dead and just leave his body there. Suddenly, he could hear someone approach. He felt the unwelcome warmth of the approaching soldier's breath and smelled the stench of sweat, tobacco and other sundries. He knew the rebel soldier was examining him to see if he was alive. Suddenly, he felt the soldier sweep backward and prepare to plunge the bayonet into him.

Instinctively, Heinrich jumped up and swept the bayonet back just within seconds.

"Well, lookie what's we got here. Not only is it a live 'bluebelly,' but it's a major," cried the confederate. "Ya'll might just come in handy as trade bait," he said, as he presented his prize find to the others. Just at that moment Heinrich felt a sharp, ripping pain in the area where he had been struck. He reached up to find a bleeding, gaping five-inch slash to the right side of his neck, where he had apparently been struck by a sword the night before. He was covered in blood from his own wound, as well as that of Henry Lyons, whose lifeless body was still lying at Heinrich's feet.

A frightened and confused, Heinrich couldn't help but wonder if he might have been better off dead as the rebels paraded him and two other officers around their ill-gotten camp. They scoffed at the three men, waved loaded rifles as if to shoot them at anytime, and spit directly in to their faces.

"...em shur is sum mighty faine calvr'y boots ya got dere Billy," one raider said to Heinrich, as he waved a sword in his face. "Dey shur wud go nice wit dis sord I took from dat officer o'er dere fer I kilt him wit it last night."

Heinrich knew what the man's intentions were and wondered if he might have enough time to reach into those same boots and grab out his pistol before being pierced by the blade.

"Wutz say ya take 'em off give 'em ta me sosst I don't gotta git 'em all bloodied," the man said.

"If you want them bad enough, try to take them, you ignorant, seccionist bastard," Heinrich said, as he spit back at the aggressor. The man immediately lunged at Heinrich in an attempt to deliver a killing blow with the sword, but Heinrich managed to shove him aside. Just at that moment a confederate colonel came on the scene and ordered the man to back off because, as an officer, Heinrich would be more value to them as a hostage.

Heinrich took a deep breath and thanked God that his life had been spared for the moment.

"I am going to have you marched to Libby Prison just as you are," the ranking officer told the prisoners. - "All torn up and bloodied. -You'll get no more mercy from me. All I want is to trade your Yankee asses for some of our own good men. But if you give me any reason, I'll kill you myself."

Heinrich was combined with other prisoners that had been gathered in raids, and some still left from the battle of Murfreesboro, a few weeks prior.

As they were marched into a Tennessee town along the way to the prison in Richmond, Va. the Yankee soldiers were viewed with curiosity, by civilians and members of the rebel, Fifty-Fourth Virginia, who laughed to see how the federal soldiers liked being hungry, tired and hopeless.

"It was the most aggravating and embarrassing way in the world to be picked up," Heinrich said later in life. "We were pounced upon by a cowardly squad of mounted ruffian guerrillas. They are not proud fighting soldiers. Just scum. We found ourselves bagged almost before we knew we were attacked and then literally dragged over the countryside like a prize they had won." He added that he would have rather been captured while facing the enemy in battle, or even killed in battle, than to end up this way.

The prisoners were furnished with a meager ration of stale bread and some unrecognizable meat, designed to last two days. Heinrich gobbled his entire supply within minutes, since he hadn't been fed in two days, and planned to fast until more food was available.

They stayed in the Murfreesboro area for about two weeks, and started for Richmond by way of Chattanooga and East Tennessee. There they were combined with all the prisoners captured at Murfreesboro-three or four thousand in number. They forded rivers, marching between the bridges, after spending days on railroad cattle cars going in multiple directions, before finally arriving in "that paradise of battle-torn prisoners, Libby Prison," Heinrich said. There, multitudes of union soldiers died everyday from battle wounds, disease, starvation, scurvy, malaria and one the main killers - dysentery.

Of all the war scenes Heinrich had witnessed and heard about, Libby had to have been among the worst, including battlefields and hospitals, he said. It was overcrowded with thousands of union soldiers. They occupied rooms that were forty-five by one hundred feet in size, with 150 prisoners in each. They slept on the floor, with only boxes and barrels for seats. Some blankets were provided by the U.S. Sanitary commission.

He saw men with every conceivable type of wound including one who had his face completely blown off in an explosion. Heinrich said the man sat in the corner by himself patiently waiting and apparently, hoping for death. He had a hole that barely resembled a mouth and no nose or eyes.

Heinrich worried of his own fate at this point, and contemplated what happened at Murfreesboro. He wondered if the 10th Ohio would realize where he was and if they would be list him as missing because he would not be found among the dead. They would probably not realize that he was taken prisoner and sent to Libby Prison because that fate was usually only for officers, which of course Heinrich was falsely still portraying, just to remain alive. Therefore, the logical conclusion of officers and men in the 10th Ohio likely was that Heinrich had become the most detestable of Civil War soldiers - a deserter! This thought bothered him greatly. Official records of the 10th Ohio Calvary do currently show him as having deserted on Feb. 14, 1863.

It was the winter of 1863 and Heinrich was locked deep in the rebel prison unable to get out and fight the war like most other 22-year-olds. Instead, he laid there every day watching as more union soldiers died and more were brought in to replace them. Major battles had taken place by then, including First and Second Bull Run (Manassas), Shiloh, Fair Oaks, Antietam (Sharpsburg) and Fredericksburg. The 83rd Pennsylvania had earned its reputation at Gaines Mills and Fredericksburg. It was at Fredericksburg, during the winter of 1862 and Chancellorsville, spring of 1863, that the confederacy had its greatest victories of the war. Even though Gen.

"Stonewall" Jackson, one of the south's greatest generals, was killed at Chancellorsville, those victories gave Gen. Robert E. Lee and his army the confidence and momentum to take the war off the Virginia peninsula and into northern territory. Lee came up with a plan to fight the union army through Pennsylvania and then head back toward Washington. D.C. This plan led to the union victory at the Battle of Gettysburg, Pa., July 1-3, 1863, which ultimately stemmed the tide of the confederacy and switched the momentum back to the north, where it would stay to the end of the war.

All of this happened while Henrich lingered in the prison with little hope of ever getting out alive. Not only was he fighting malnutrition and dysentery constantly, but worse, the sword wound to his neck was infected and resulted in a large ball that oozed puss constantly, leaving a six inch gap exposed. He managed to keep it clean with the small amounts of water he had and even tried some medications that he had come by, but his only temporary relief was to lance the wound and drain it daily. It was causing him great headaches and often left him greatly weakened physically and mentally.

Union prisoners were provided only rudimentary medical attention. Only those with minor wounds to the limbs had any serious chance at survival. As was common practice throughout the Civil War, both at the hands of friendly and enemy surgeons, it was quicker, more practical and thought-to-be more life saving, to saw off a wounded limb rather than treat many wounds. An enormous stack of limbs, hands and feet lay in heaps only a few feet outside where Heinrich was being held. One of his duties was to carry out dead union soldiers each day and bury them.

One of the few positives that Heinrich experienced in Libby Prison was that he used to see the confederate guards playing a strange game that involved bases and a ball. An offensive player would strike the thrown ball with a club or a bat and then try to reach the base before the defending players caught the ball to "get him out." Heinrich's curiosity and fascination with the game got the best of him one day and he asked one of the guards what the game was. "I think they call it Rounders," explained Confederate Sgt. Alexander R. Hensel, from Atlanta, "We've been playing it for years. I think it evolved from an old English game," he said.

"But, then I better not tell Ya'll to much about it before Ya'll go home and tell them damned Yankees about it and they're beating us at that too."

The food was poor, miserable and deluded, often consisting only of unbolted cornmeal at best, which was corn that was ground husk and all. It was normally fed to livestock. They were given small amounts of meat and vegetables that were barely recognizable. Henrich longed for freedom from the filth, vermon and stench. His thoughts were almost always on home or something palatable to eat, something respectable to wear and a comfortable, protected place to sleep. But most of all, he wondered how close he might be to death between his wound and all the other factors. He worried of dying in that place and disgracing his family by never having faced-off against the enemy in actual battle. Or, worse, he worried of dying and never even having his family know about it all.

Undoubtedly, the happiest men on the battlefields of the Civil War were those who suffered a disabling wound, usually to a limb. Even though the injury usually resulted in amputation, the soldier was allowed to escape the battle and be sent home with their wound as an "emblem of courage," having spent a minimum amount of time lingering in a hospital.

Of the still-living, the most unhappy soldiers were the severly wounded and those taken prisoner. It didn't take Civil War soldiers, from either side, long to realize that it was almost better to die a quick death on the battlefield rather than linger and suffer in a hospital or prison, facing eventual death. They claimed it took more courage to lie in the hospital facing inevitable death than to have it happen in the heat of battle. The feelings were similar when it came to being held in a prison camp, but what made that even worse is the shame and embarrassment of being taken alive by the enemy and completely at their mercy.

Heinrich's one hope was that he could become subject to the parole and prisoner exchange system which existed during the first years of the war. An officer would sign a prepared statement to the effect of: "I give my word of honor as an officer and a gentlemen that I will not bear arms or exercise any of the functions of my office under my commision from the President of the United States, against the Confederate States of America, during the existence of the war between the said confederate and United States, unless I shall be exhanged for another prisoner or prisoners of war, or unless I shall be released by the President of the Confederate States."

The enlisted man promised never to take arms against the Confederate States, nor give any aid and comfort to the United States against the Confederacy during the war unless exchanged or released.

CHAPTER 6

ESCAPED SLAVE SAVES HIS LIFE

B y spring of 1863 Heinrich made his mind up that he was not going to wait to be exchanged and that he was not going to die in that despicable place. He planned with a hand full of other prisoners to attempt an escape. On a selected night they all volunteered to carry the latest casualties to the "dead house." They pulled-off their escape as they were able to over-power a couple of guards and make their escape into the Virginia woodlands.

Their getaway was almost too easy, Heinrich said. Once they were past the guards they overcame a few walls and then were virtually able to walk off the prison grounds. They were not concerned about being followed or tracked by dogs right away because it was the middle of the night and they felt assured they had escaped undetected. But they still hurried to put as much time and space between them and the prison as they could.

Heinrich bathed in his new found freedom. Even though they were still deep in enemy territory, he relished the spring warmth and lush green natural beauty that was such a welcome contrast to the gray starkness of the prison pen. His first thoughts were of freedom from the enemy and getting back to join the 10th Ohio Calvary, but then he worried if they might not accept his explanation of taking the major's jacket to save his life. If he could not convince them and account for his time away from the unit for the past few months he would be branded a coward, ridiculed and possibly executed for desertion. So as he scurried north he wondered if he might just be rushing to death at the hands of his own comrades.

The four men hastened to find friendly troops. They travelled by night and slept by day. However, as Heinrich's luck would have it, one night they stumbled into a Confederate camp. They looked in all directions only to realize that they were practically surrounded by Confederates. Heinrich began to panic when he thought they might have to find an escape around the enormous encampment in northern Virginia. Suddenly, he heard a familiar buzzing sound wip past his ear. He had little time to react, or alert his friends before he saw two of them fall dead from confederate minie balls.

He felt a sudden burning sensation in his right shoulder and sickening feeling in his stomach. He fought the urge to collapse as he felt a heavy hand grab for him. He reached for his pistol and began to sweep around when a deep voice spoke in the darkness.

"Holt on der Yank. Don't ya'll yells out and get scare't. I is here to help git you away from these rebels."

Heinrich shaded his eyes from the moonlight but all he could see was a large pair of white eyes. Then a large row of white teeth appeared surrounded by a warming smile. "Don't make no noise. Juss run wiff me. I'll takes ya ta safedy." the deep voice said.

Heinrich followed the enormous figure as they scurried through the woods and brush, for what seemed liked hours. When they finally had a chance to stop by a brook, Heinrich could see in the early morning light that his "savior" was the largest Negro he had ever seen.

"You'z Yanks ken call me Josef. I runs de unner grount railroat in dis area. I scaped from my masser long time ago. Now I helps Yanks and scaped slaves gets to dey freedom. Dis here woods is teaming wif runaway slaves and too many confedrits. Every now and den I comes across some bluebellys in a fix like you."

Josef told the men that Gen. Lee and his approximately 75,000 soldiers were spread over the northern Virginia countryside trying to make their way in to Pennsylvania in an apparent major offensive attack on the Northern Army of the Potomac. In order for Heinrich to rejoin the 10th Ohio Calvary he would either have to head back south around the Confederate army, and then through western Virginia and into the Kentucky/Tennesee areas, or head north in to lower Pennsylvania, which is the direction the confederates were headed, and down to hopefully meet his unit, if they were still in southern Tennessee.

The men agreed the best way would be to join some escaped slaves and follow the underground railroad north until it was safe to head west through lower Pennsylvania. By going that route, Heinrich could make a choice continue on to meet the 10th Ohio or hook up with the Northern Army of the Potomac, which was the main fighting body of the union.

As they sat by a warm campfire the night after Josef came to their rescue, Heinrich stared directly at the enormous Negro as he told the Union soldiers what life was like for slaves. Heinrich saw bulging muscles and what appeared to be a healthy middle-aged man. Heinrich asked his age and was shocked when Josef approximated it at only 29 years old.

" Dis is what slafery does to a human," Josef relayed. Heinrich's interest at that point turned almost to a frightenting curiousity. He stared deep into big, blood shot eyes and could see the pain, suffering and sacrifices the man had made in a lifetime that was only a few years longer than his own. Heinrich's own eyes swelled and flowed with tears as he looked down the man's tortured frame in more detail. He saw scars and dried, sun-baked skin from decades of hard toil in the plantation's cotton fields. He saw distorted, twisted fingers and hands. But Heinrich's eyes locked as they approached the man's right foot.

"Dey call dat my club foot," Josef said, not seeming to be disturbed at all by Heinrich's frightened stare. "De oerseer did dat ta me the second time I trite to escape. Affer dey dogs hunted me down he took a board and tied it between my two ankles and slammed on the de outside my right foot wif a hammer."

'This here is one damned nigger boy who will never run again,' the oerseer said, "while de others stood around laughing at my agony."

At that point Josef stood, turned around and steadily peeled off what remained of a tattered cotton shirt. Heinrich stared uncomfortably as he watched fibers of the shirt adhearing to scars, dead skin and bleeding areas that never healed properly. "De oerseer gave me a lashin after the first time I ranaway," Josef continued, but none of what he did to my body is as bad as what de did the third time I ran."

It took six of em to holt me back, and they made me watch, while they all raped my twelve-year-old daughter. They then dragged her off an I wasn't sure if she was alive, or not. Next day I begged my masser to tell me if my little LuLu was still alive. All he would tell me is that it was time for LuLu to be sold to another plantation."

Josef told Heinrich that it was then that he made up his mind to attempt his fourth, and ultimately successful escape. "I jus figgered at that point ain't nothin else dey could do, or take from me, dat could hurt that much," he said. "Even though they said I couldn't run, I ran faster den ever before, and when I stopped I hat gone even further den ever and den I ran sum mo for my little girl. I didn't let no pain bother me none. I've been runnin eva sense."

Das why I runs dis railroat. I knows my LuLu's got my spirit, and ifin she's alive, she's gonna run someday too. I want her to take dis railroat right in to her daddy's waitin arms."

Josef continued, "Dat manicipation procamation Mssr Linkum issued back on January 1st of this year ain't freet a single slave cuss the soufff juss set, 'Hell wiff you, we at war anyway. We ain't gonna abide by your rules.'"

Heinrich used his knees to support his elbows as he cupped his hands over his face and for the first time in more than twenty years he cried uncontrollably.

Henrich had known many Negroes while growing up in Erie but never paid them much attention. Typical of many citizens in the north, he was sickened at the thought of slavery, but didn't necessarily consider his fight to free them until now.

"Well afore you go rejoinin the Yankees and freeing de slaves, ya'll bess let me dig dat minie ball out yer shoulder," Josef said, realizing that Heinrich had taken a serious wound the night before. Josef noticed that Heinrich was still nursing his neck wound from the raid and now had another one to contend with. He had been fighting the infection from the previous wound and will probably have the same problem with the shoulder, Josef said. He added that Heinrich would probably not have enough time and strength left in him to reach his unit before the infections killed him. "An even if you do reach em, de army surgin only gonna saw dat arm off anyway. It's quicker and easier den operatin wif all da soldiers de got to care for now," Josef said.

"Yeah, but then I can go right back home to Erie and tell them I'm disabled hero," Heinrich joked.

Josef told him that his best chance of surviving was to make it to a friend of his who lives just outside of Baltimore, Md. His friend Amelia is an escaped slave who smuggles slaves across the Mason Dixon line to their freedom in the northern states. "Dey calls her a witch doctor," Josef explained. She has remedies to many illnesses and conditions "dat evin da bess white doctors ain't no where near discoverin yet."

She uses a combination of mold, herbs and some other ingredients that she grows around her property. She can cure an infection in days, he said.

"Soldiers on both sides die every day from infections," Heinrich responded.

The next day Heinrich and the only other surviving escapee from Libby joined Josef and a hand full of escaped slaves on the route through northern Virginia into Maryland.

One day when all the others were comfortably asleep Heinrich and Josef went out to forage for some food along the Virginia countryside.

Suddenly a strong demanding voice cracked through the silence, "Stay right there Bluebelly 'cuss I'm fixin to blow your nigger's head off and scatter the little bit of brains he has all over Ya'll."

Heinrich looked up to see a young confederate picket with his rifle pressed against the side of Josef's head. "Now just ease that cavalry pistol out slowly and pass it to me," the private said. Heinrich responded, "I don't think it's gonna make a good collector's item Johnny because I'm still looking to kill my first rebel with it."

The soldier did not seem to appreciate Heinrich's humor. "I'm just followin' my orders to kill runaway niggers and then give yanks a choice. I will kill you here or take you prisoner."

"Who would of given you an order like that,?" Heinrich questioned.

"I reckon a general thunk it up," was the response.

"I can assure you it was no respectful general like Robert E. Lee or "Ol' Pete" (Conf. Gen. James Peter Longstreet)," Heinrich said. "Are you telling me you take your orders from a bushwhacking, renegade officer Johnny, come on, I can tell you're smarter than that."

"I tell you what though since you are intent on shooting Josef, at least let me step out from behind him because I'm afraid the way you're shaking that you might miss his head and hit mine," Heinrich said. " I can tell right now you're more afraid than I am and you're the one holding the rifle, Johnny.

"How old you?

"You're only a Babe!

"What's your name,?" Heinrich questioned.

"I'm twenty-three and my name is Shamus Harwood," the confederate said.

"Nah! You're shaken so bad you can't remember your age boy."

"Ok, I'll be 17 on July 3 of this year,"

"Your Irish, Right Shamus? Well, I'm second-generation German. Here we are, both dragged into this damned war that should be none of our business. Where are you from Shamus?"

"I'm from Alabamy. My daddy was a sharecropper and his daddy before him."

"How many slaves do own?"

"Only the rich people own slaves."

"So your family's life is only slightly better than the negroe's, huh Shamus?"

Shamus thought for a second, took a deep reflective pause and wiped the perspiration from his quivering brow.

"Why are you and all these 'good ol' boys' fighting us," Shamus?

"We're protectin' ooouur rots," Shamus replied in his best southern accent.

"Brother, what rights of yours have we threatened?"

Shamus scratched his head, managed a slight relaxed smile in Heinrich's direction and then looked at the ground for a few seconds. Heinrich glanced into the deep woods and listened as a woodpecker pounded away at his new home only a few feet away, apparently oblivious to what was transpiring.

Heinrich suddenly gleamed skyward and said, "Thank you God." This startled Shamus back to the conversation as he quizzically replied, "I don't really know, but when I find out, I reckon I'll be fightin' for those rots too."

"Do you want to remain a sharecropper your whole life Shamus?"

"No, people always told me I have a knack for writing. I want to go to one of those big fancy New York City journalism schools someday," Shamus replied.

" HHHAAAAAAHH, So yer a Yankee at heart ain't you boy."

" Guess it depends on how you look at it," Shamus answered slowly.

Heinrich smiled and eased closer to Shamus. "My brother I'm going to give you a chance to save Josef's life and your own too. You see, you've been shaking so bad you knocked the cap off your rifle that's why I just thanked the Lord. If you pull that trigger right now the only sound, and the last sound you will ever hear will be metal striking metal, there will be no spark to ignite your powder," Heinrich continued.

"Because if you reach in your pouch for another cap I will reach in my boot at same time for my knife and drive it deep into your heart before you can pull the trigger again.

Put the rifle down, Johnny Reb and let's talk some more, instead."

Shamus lowered the rifle, slumped against a tree and cried aloud, "I failed in my duty."

"No Shamus, you did the right thing. God directed you, not some rich, arrogant general who could care less about your life, mine or anybody else's.

"Think about it, how can these rich white southerners who claim to be fighting to protect their rights be so hypocritical as to enslave another man and steal all of his rights just to benefit themselves?

"I think if somebody wants to make a slave of another man, they ought to try it on him first. As people are saying – ' Its a rich man's war, but a poor man's fight,' Heinrich said.

"You go to that fancy New York school someday, Shamus. And then you write yourself a book about this dirty, disgustin' war. Don't write about the battles and the generals and their strategies and accomplishments. They're not the heroes --- you are!

Tell the world what war is. It's the murder of innocents everybody suffers. The glory is an illusion. It's only those who have never seen battle who want more of it."

He continued, " Write that book Shamus and maybe someday you, me and good ol' Josef can meet someplace -- maybe someplace like New York --- and we can cry and brag about what heroes and fools we were."

CHAPTER 7

NEAR DEATH IN BALTIMORE AGAIN

Heinrich and Josef slowly and steadily moved their way north toward Amelia's with a number of escaped slaves following. But, each day Heinrich's condition was worsening from the wounds to his right shoulder and neck. The pain from the infection was too much for him to tolerate at times and he even begged Josef to cut his arm off at the shoulder.

Josef pleaded with Heinrich to endure the pain a few days longer because Amelia would hopefully be able to heal the wound and infection.

Finally, only less than two days away from Baltimore Heinrich fell to his knees and yelled to Josef that they had two choices, either perform the rugged surgery, or leave him there to die while the others continued. Just as he barked the ultimatum to Josef he felt his perspiring, pain-filled, body slam to the ground. Then just as swiftly he felt a rising, lifting movement as he was swept up by the powerful black arms of Josef.

Heinrich's next conscious sense was one of comfort and an atmosphere that he had not experienced since the day he left home two years prior.

JAMES J. CONNELL, JR.

He felt himself perspiring and pulsating slightly, but then a sudden cooling gentle hand graced his forehead and face.

Mother, he managed, while keeping his eyes still tightly closed. He paused in silence for a second fearing that if he opened his eyes the first image would not be his mother and the pain would return.

" Nooooohhh, I is not yo momma, boy, but I tryin' to take care of you like she wut," a comforting voice replied.

Heinrich slowly opened his eyes and saw a dark, shriveled loving woman staring directly down at him. Her gentle,wrinkled face was framed softly by a mass of bright white hair that was tightly pulled back.

He moved his right fingers to see if the arm and hand were still there. He could feel a soft mattress and a warm blanket against his body. He felt their comfort, the likes of which he hadn't known in years. He felt a warm in the room and smelled fresh food and baked goods. He had forgotten just how much he missed these small things.

" You must be Amelia," Heinrich said. " Das right," she replied.

" You was in real bat shape when Josef carriet you in here more than a week ago. I thought I was gonna lose you 'bout five days ago, but my medicine worked again," Amelia said, as she reached for a crusty spittoon and hurled a jet of tobacco juice dead center.

"They call you a witch doctor. Did you perform voodoo and bring me back from the dead,?" Heinrich asked as he clung the blankets closer to his chest and backed away concerned his question might cause anger and she would get revenge by casting a spell.

" Dey kin calls me what dey wants, Lordy knows I bin callt worse. But if dey knew to mix the herbs the moss and the molds da way I do, der be a whole lot fewer boys like you dieing every day from infections," Amelia replied. She hurled another spray into the spittoon and yelped for someone named Cylus to get in there right away.

"Why don't you let doctors know about your cures,? Heinrich asked. " I tright. Ain't nobody who wants to listen to no igrint, ol' nigger woman, is wut dey tells me. So I juss helps da people I can."

"Maddam, You are a saint and as long as I am alive, I shall regard you as such," Heinrich responded.

At that point Amelia informed Heinrich of a great, pending battle that was due to take place in neighboring Pennsylvania sometime during early July. Conf. Gen. Robert E. Lee has more than 50,000 troops making their way in to that area so they can strike a blow at the heart of the Army of the Potomac, Amelia told him, based on what freed negroes in the area were saying.

If they are successful from there, they can stroll right through Baltimore and rally that city to join the Confederacy and then continue on to Washington and the capital will be all theirs, Heinrich added.

Suddenly, a boy about 12 years old interrupted and burst in to the small room.

"Fetch me my cane Cylus and while you're at it, get dis Yankee a fresh drink of colt water," Amelia barked. The boy handed the old lady a crude stick and she slowly propped herself up. Heinrich was shocked to see that she was missing her right leg.

Heinrich barely realized just how thirsty he was until the cold water soothed so nicely. "That was great son, can you manage a little more,? Heinrich asked.

He noted that the negroe boy was a dirty half-naked creature who stood barefoot and looked like he didn't care if he ever took a bath again. Yet, he seemed mysteriously calm and well-behaved, unlike descriptions of negroe children that Heinrich had heard from many white people.

Heinrich remembered that he had three cents in his pocket that he tucked away in prison camp in case he needed it to bribe a guard. He thought that a penny for each Ameilia and Cylus would show a small token of appreciation.

He reached for Amelia's small, frail hand and pressed the penny in her soft palm. He noted how her fingers seemed disjointed and appeared crippled in multiple directions. Amelia gleamed a shy, gracious, mostly-toothless smile and thanked Heinrich. He then turned to the boy and noted an odd-looking, dark, dirtied hat that he was wearing which seemed much too small for his growing head. He thought it was strange that the boy had been in the room for nearly five minutes and hadn't uttered a word, not even to Amelia.

Heinrich slowly reached for the hat and tried to indicate to the lad that he was going toss a penny into it. Suddenly, the boy thrashed at Heinrich's arm, knocking the penny across the room. He grasped tightly to his hat and thrust it against his chest with both hands and ran screaming out of the house.

" Get back here boy, what's wrong with you? I was offering to throw a small gift in your hat," Heinrich yelled. " Madam that is crude behavior if ever I've seen such and a belligerent act such as that requires that you whip that welp," he added.

" If that's what you wants masser I will whip him right now, but afor I do, will you allow me to esplain somethin'."

Amelia calmly began;

"You see, when he was a young boy, his masser got angry one day at the boy's daddy. The masser tolt the ooeerseer ta punish his family. De ooeerseer got drunk and set fire to dey house. Da boy tright to fight de ooeerseer and save his mommy and daddy but de both burned up in the fire along with five children.

" Next day, in da rubble all the boy fount was his little hat. He stole a gun from de masser's house and walked up to the ooeerser and shot him square between the eyes. Fore the oooeerseer fell dead, da boy threw the gun and was already runnin' away.

Days later, Josef found him naked, cold and alone, clutching his hat. He's been wif me ever since. He helps me bring slaves to dey freedom up norf.

"You see, Dat hat is de only thing he owns and you is one of few white men he has seen since de oooeerseer. He has never met a white person who has been nice to him.

He didn't mean no disrespect but I'll go whip him severely for ya now if you still wants," Amelia said.

Heinrich lunged to stop her and pulled her close to his chest as he cried, " Please God, if you would be so kind as to forgive my ignorance."

The next day Amelia told Heinrich that if he would help her guide some escaped slaves across the Mason Dixon to freedom in the North that she would help guide him back past the Confederate Army to Union lines.

As they were preparing for the trip from Maryland into eastern Pennsylvania Heinrich watched as Amelia meticulously stuffed her small two-wheeled cart with many articles of clothing. There were many colorful, decorative articles and garments that appeared to be professionally created, and which obviously, only the very wealthy could afford. Immediately, a family of runaway slaves presented themselves to Amelia.

Amelia pointed to two adults and three children and explained to Heinrich, "Da small ones I hide in my cart. Da big ones go up under my dress til we gets to safedy.

After I get da slaves to freedom I continue on to New York City where da merchants take the clothing I make and sells it to da rich people. Dey gives me a little money and more scraps so I can make more clothes. "Dats how I help more people to dey freedom."

Heinrich's grueling trek that began during February 1863 in Murfreesboro and led him deep in to Virginia was now leading him through Maryland and back into his home state. His plan was to escort Amelia and the refugees to safety and then head back to the Tennessee area in hopes of locating the 10th Ohio Cavalry.

Within days the group was about to cross the border into Pennsylvania when a stranger approached Amelia. He was a filthy-looking individual with ragged, torn clothes. His face drooped to one side exposing blackened, decayed stubs of what apparently were teeth that had been eaten away by decades of neglect and chewing tobacco. His unkempt, matted, whiskers were caked with tobacco stains that soaked to his skin, down his neck and slopped on his shredded clothing.

"How's bout you give me a drink of cold water old nigger lady,?" the stranger belched. Amelia slowly and cautiously reached for a canteen that she had slung over her shoulder when the stranger suddenly lunged at her and grabbed her frail arm.

"My name is John. I'm the boss around here," as if that was supposed to impress and intimidate Amelia.

"Now I ain't talkin about that warm water dats bin danglin' on yer hip. I want cold water that's hid under all those rags," he said, as he grabbed some articles of clothing and flung them to the ground.

"Please masser don't wrinkle my clothes da rich people will be upset," Amelia begged, but she really knew what the man was looking for.

Suddenly, the man straightened up and bloated an obnoxious laugh. "Ah Hah nigger woman I gots you at last. I see a passell full of little nigger slaves in dis here cart.

"Dey shur is gonna make me a mighty fine bounty when I gets them back to their owners. And, now you, cuss you committed dis crime I can sell you back in to slavery. What do ya thinks I can get for a crafty ol' nigger woman like you?, the man asked, as he reached out and groped her breasts and slowly worked his way down her hips.

He then yanked at the canteen and bent to steal a swig as Amelia lowered her face to meet his and promptly spit an enormous jet of tobacco juice directly in to his eyes. He groped for his rifle, but before he could grab it, Amelia slammed her cane as hard as she could deep in to his groin.

As the man was slumping to the ground Amelia caught him and suspended him by a greasy clump of hair.

"I always said I wouldn't give a cold drink of water to a bounty hunter even as he was about to take his last breath," Amelia said. "And you, worthless lowlife, are no exception to that rule."

With that a shot rang out from underneath Amelia's dress and drilled the bounty hunter right between the eyes.

Heinrich rolled out from under her dress laughing, "Finally, this revolver has seen some much needed action," he said.

"I was handling it myself," Amelia said.

"Yeah, but you were slow and taking too long," Heinrich responded.

"That's the way bounty hunters are supposed to die," Amelia added.

CHAPTER 8

GETTYSBURG NIGHTMARE

Once the escaped slaves reached their freedom, Heinrich bid an emotional farewell to the woman who saved his life, and vowed that he would see her again some day when the country is re-united and "no man, woman or child is held in bondage."

He headed west in lower Pennsylvania, and once again felt the severe pain of being alone and victimized by this cruel war. He still suffered from the after-affects of his wounds, especially from being shot in the shoulder. He resigned himself to the fact that he would have minimal control or strength in his right arm and likely never be able to raise it above his shoulder. As he walked along the arm painfully dangled and cramped up. He cried aloud at the haunting thought that he may never be able to lift and fire a rifle once he re-joined the Union Army.

The early-July weather made his trek difficult also. One day was scorching, then, the next day would bring a downpour. As he trudged along, Heinrich spotted an old man struggling to push a wagon out of some mud. The person sitting up front lashed at the pitiful horse as the man pried to no avail. Without hesitating, Heinrich grabbed a sturdy branch and angled it under a wheel. Within minutes the vehicle was freed.

"I want to thank you 'Billy Yank', but I really have nothing left to share," the old man said, as he reached his muddy hand out to shake Heinrich's. "The only money my daughter and I had we spent renting this rig. We came down from Troy, New York to go to this place they call 'Giddesburg' and retrieve my only son."

" I read in the *Troy Record* newspaper that on the third day of fighting my boy fell in with a Troy unit, the 125th New York Regimental Volunteers. They say them boys from Troy, mostly Irish and German decent, fought proud, and hard defending some rock wall in the middle of nowhere against some secessionist general named Pickett and his Virginia boys," the old man said.

He slowly removed his humble slouch hat and tearfully looked skyward.

"Them Troy boys fought the good fight. The leaders ordered them not to give an inch and don't let them 'Johnnies' cross that wall. Now this country is celebrating this great victory they earned, while me, and a whole lot of other parents are left to make our way down here to bring their bodies back home for proper burial."

"This may be abrupt, sir, but, I would be so honored if you would allow to me to ride along with you and help you finish your mission," Heinrich said.

"You would do that for us? You've helped us already, and obviously sacrificed enough in this war," came a soft, feminine voice from the driver's seat. He took what seemed like minutes to recover and struggled to focus his worn eyes on the source.

Slowly, the most beautiful sight he had ever seen, and certainly the nicest he had seen since the war began, came in to focus.

His eyes immediately met hers and he felt drawn in and mesmerized by their bright beauty. Her long, light brown hair was parted in the middle and gently cascaded to her shoulders, framing her petite face perfectly. As she held her steady stare at Heinrich, over her small wire eyeglasses, he felt almost as if he could read her mind. He fought the urge to leap over the wagon rail and just sweep her up in a loving embrace.

He noticed in the middle of the part in her hair there was a small clump of very white hair that stood out, yet seemed to blend smoothly and gave her a mature, distinguished look.

She appeared to be a few years younger than Heinrich, yet more mature and confident. He could tell she was far from being a pampered child and apparently has had to work hard her entire life with chores and the affairs of family.

"My name is Mary Miller," she smiled, while gently extending her hand to meet his.

"Heinrich Thibaut," he choked, as he searched for more words to say to her while maintaining the stare. "My,my,my name is HHHHeinrich - HHHHHeinrich TTTThibaut he stuttered.

"I heard you the first time, Heinrich. You are German, the same as me," Mary said. "YYYYes" he said, wishing that he could talk as confidently as she was. "My father is a laborer from Erie, Pennsylvania," he said.

As he reluctantly released her gentle grasp, he clumsily fell in to the horse that was attached to the wagon, causing the horse to bolt forward and pull the wagon over his right foot. He fell flat on his back in to deep mud, not so much from the pain in his foot, but from his own awkward clumsiness.

Mary jolted from the wagon directly in to the nearly, knee-deep mud and yelled for Heinrich to lift his leg up so she could remove his brogan and tend to his apparent foot injury. Heinrich started to tell Mary that the foot was not harmed because the wheel merely forced it down harmlessly in to the thick soft mud. But Mary worked so swiftly and decisively that he had no opportunity, or, at least, he decided not to take the opportunity, to stop her.

Heinrich tried not to laugh aloud as he held the secret in because Mary seemed so determined to doctor him and he was enjoying the attention. She removed a small scarf from her shoulder and wrapped it tightly around his foot. Heinrich could tell the way she worked that she's tended to many injuries in her life.

"Quickly father, help me lift young Heinrich in to our wagon, we've injured him now he must continue to Gettysburg as my patient."

Mary threw Heinrich's left arm around her soft neck as her father grabbed under his right shoulder. Heinrich absorbed the majority of his weight so as not to strain the frail beauty or her elderly father. He seated himself firmly in the bed of the wagon and grimaced and groaned slightly to make his little ruse appear believable.

With this, the trio set out for Gettysburg, which was still a full day's ride ahead. Heinrich enjoyed the chance to ride in a vehicle for the first time in years, but more than that he relished the attention he was getting from Mary. For the first time in his life, he was steadily falling in love.

They were a few hours from their destination when Mary asked Heinrich if she may have a turn lying in the bed of the small wagon. Shortly after they exchanged places Heinrich noticed that she was sleeping soundly in the afternoon sun.

Heinrich turned to his left and looked at Mr. Miller as the old man was driving the wagon. He thought for a second and pursed his lips tightly inward. He tightened his upper body and looked down as he uttered a confession. "My foot is really unharmed, sir, it merely sunk in the mud, you needn't worry over me."

"I knew that all along, son, he responded. "And, ya know something, if I'm readin' Mary's mind right, she knew it too. But, she's also thinkin' other thoughts. I know better than to interfere with Mary when she's made her mind up. So you proceed careful-like and we'll be all right," the man warned. "You know what I mean."

This encouraged Heinrich, yet scared him at the same time. Was he ready for love and its responsibilities given his situation?

"Why ain't you over with General Meade and the rest of the Union Army," the man asked. Heinrich told him of his situation and escaping from the confederate prison. "I'm gonna join the fight as soon as I can, sir, he said, hoping the man would not consider him a coward.

But Heinrich's confidence began to waver as they neared Gettysburg. Even though it had been nearly a week since the great fight, Heinrich could see clouds of smoke billowing from uncontrolled fires remaining in the distant battlefields. Their darkness hung over the area and made the others sights even bleaker. He saw throngs of wagons carrying bodies out of the city. Some wagons contained many wounded soldiers piled in heaps. He could hear the shouts and cries of the wounded as the wagons traversed over the rough roads. There were some soldiers slowly progressing on foot, many helping each other, and some using the rifles as makeshift canes and walking sticks.

There were crude hospital tents and, shelters scattered all over the area. The tents were surrounded by heaps of wounded and dying soldiers from both sides, while volunteers worked feverishly to tend to them. The hospital areas looked more like butcher houses, Heinrich thought, because they were spattered with blood and all had enormous piles of feet, hands, limbs and body parts.

The worse part was the horrible stench, Heinrich said. It emanated from the entire city of Gettysburg. This was the smell of rotting bodies and horrible unsanitary conditions. Volunteers were flooding in to help, but their challenge seemed so ghastly and monumental he thought.

Just as they entered the city a man who appeared to be a doctor waved them to a halt. He wore an outfit that was so covered in blood that the white was barely discernible. His ungloved hands were covered in blood and his hair was matted with it.

"If you're going over to the battlefield I strongly urge that the young lady shall remain here with us," the doctor said to Mary's father. "Certainly the experiences over there will be too much for the frail child that she may be tainted forever."

Before her father could react, Mary yelled to the doctor that she was there to assist her father with the retrieval of her brother and that she was not going to allow anything to stand in her way. She added that she had much experience tending to wounds and injuries and had witnessed death close up many times.

"You have never witnessed death such as this though, madam," the man said. "Sir, I beg you don't let the child go to the battlefield. As you can see, she could be more helpful to us here with the wounded, while you, and the apparently very-capable soldier complete your chore."

Mary looked at her father and glanced toward Heinrich in hopes of some support for her cause. "Go Mary. I'll retrieve you on the way back. You'll serve a better purpose here," her father said. At that, she reluctantly exited the wagon and asked the doctor where she could start to work.

The two men continued about a mile into town and merely had to follow the thickening stream of dead and wounded soldiers to tell where the heart of the fighting was.

They stopped a young soldier who appeared capable, and Mr. Miller asked, "They say my boy can be found at the area they call 'The Angle,' could you direct me young man." Heinrich looked down into the boy's eyes as he slowly lifted his head. He appeared to be about Heinrich's age but his darkened skin seemed old and crusted making him look nearly 40-years-old. His features were barely discernible because his face was masked in a combination of blood and black gun powder.

His tattered uniform was so badly damaged that they could not tell if he was union or confederate. As his head fell back to acknowledge them, his cap slipped back on his head revealing a large crop of dirtied, blond hair that appeared to be falling out in clumps.

The boy looked up at the pair and desperately squinted to bring them into focus. Heinrich thought to himself that it appeared the boy hadn't tried to focus at anything for days. He silently wondered what the last sight was that the soldier may have witnessed. The soldier's hands and face shook as he tried to speak. He raised a grizzled hand to block the sun from his eyes.

"KKKKKin, KKKKin you please, SPSPspare a DRDRDRdrink of water, SSSSir,?" the boy begged as his whole body trembled. Heinrich rapidly grabbed a canteen and held it to the lad's mouth as he desperately used his hands to shovel as much water as he could into his mouth and on to his face. The soldier guzzled the water as a wild animal would while struggling to preserve its life.

He then stepped back and raised his trembling right arm. He made no attempt to steady it as he pointed and whispered, "Over there. Clump of trees. WWWWall." He then turned with streams of water cleaning a path down his face, and stared for a moment before waving them goodbye.

As they approached the area of the already-infamous, "Pickett's Charge," Miller told Heinrich that he would prefer to be alone as he searched the immediate area for his son. He said he would let Heinrich know when he needed help and the two agreed to meet later at that same spot.

Heinrich saw this as an opportunity to seek out the areas known as 'Little Round Top' and 'The Devil's Den,' where he had heard The 83rd Pennsylvania, with many soldiers from his hometown, had fought valiantly.

He took hours to traverse the mile-long distance to the two points through the most gruesome scenes he could have ever imagined.

Later in life he would write of that experience:

AFTER THE FIGHT

"If Hell has a face, the aftermath of battle is what it would look like.
There are thousands of soldiers from both sides strewn in
every imaginable distorted configuration all over the field.
Most are dead, but surprisingly many wounded lay scattered.
Some lie patiently, waiting for help, while others are
begging and pleading for water, food or just assistance.
"Many of the wounded seem to be just laying there resigned
to an ultimate death. Sadly, they are staring at pictures of
loved ones and some are even attempting to scrawl notes and
letters. Volunteers feverishly work to save lives while covering

their faces with cloths treated with various solutions in an
effort to shield their nostrils from the horrid stench.
"I offered my assistance as I could, which led me to discover many
horrific scenes, some of which were almost too unbelievable for words.
"I came across many soldiers stretched out flat on their backs
with their rifles poised under their chins, and either a finger,
or in some cases, a toe, on the trigger. They apparently decided
their pain was too much to bear and took their own lives.
I came across many cases of living, wounded
soldiers pinned under masses of dead.
"In almost every case the dead laid with pockets turned out from
thieves and scavengers seeking money or valuables. The saddest part
was many personal mementos such as pictures, letters and trinkets
were recklessly strewn on the ground with wanton disregard.
"Many articles of uniforms, weapons and accoutrements were removed by
scavengers and souvenir hunters who raked over the battlefields within
minutes of the end of the fighting. In some cases, soldiers laid naked,
completely stripped of anything that might have the remotest value.
"Once again, I saw wild pigs ripping at remains and even
saw one union officer desperately fighting back the pigs as
they ripped at what remained of his wounded legs.
"If you were to ask me, I would say that the politicians and generals
who wage these wars should be made to walk the battlefield
afterwards to see what their efforts have really wrought.
"I couldn't help but think to myself that this is the ultimate
fate for these brave dedicated soldiers who fought so nobly for
their cause – this is the respect they are given in the end.

Heinrich slowly tediously made his way across the field to the
southern slope of Little Round Top and the exact spot where Col.
Strong Vincent had fallen. He looked across and saw that many bodies
still lay there, including many from Erie and the 83 Pennsylvania. As he
slowly made his way down toward where he figured the 83rd men were,

he spotted the familiar face of a confederate soldier, with a deadened stare glaring right up at him. Upon closer inspection he realized that the soldier was Sgt. Alexander Hensel, the guard from Libby Prison. "I will never forget those cold, frozen eyes, staring right at me," he said.

He then made his way to a mass of union dead where he did find members of the 83rd. He was hoping not to find any familiar faces, but unfortunately he did recognize some of the boys who he grew up with in Erie and soldiers he knew from the old Erie Regiment.

But the find that bothered Heinrich most was an old friend, Sgt. Duane B. Fish. Fish was wearing a Union Kepi cap and sack coat but the rest was civilian attire. Heinrich knew his friend was not a member of the 83rd, but had apparently rushed to Gettysburg to meet the boys from Erie once he heard the confederates were entering his home state of Pennsylvania. Heinrich turned the body over and counted at least six bullet holes.

He held the body tight as he cried and thought about Fish's proud heritage.

During the 1840s in Erie, Heinrich remembers Fish as an elderly, war veteran full of stories. Fish never really knew how old he was. All he knew was he was born on the Fourth of July, "a few years after the birth of our great country in 1776." He served during the War of 1812 and the Mexican War in the mid-1840s. Soldiering was the only life that Fish ever knew, according to what he used to tell Heinrich, and he yearned for more of it, despite his age and various wounds. Fish had many scars on his chest from bullet and knife wounds he suffered in previous wars and Heinrich remembered how the old timer never had full use of his right arm and shoulder from battle injuries.

"Yer only as old as you feel. I can keep up with any 20-year-old," Fish often said. Heinrich estimated that the fallen hero had to be in his 70s.

The more Heinrich thought about Fish and the others, the more he cried, and the angrier he got.

He grabbed the fallen hero with both hands on his collar and pulled his face up even with his own. He stared right into the dead expression and screamed, "Why Fish? Why, Why, Why are we doing this? Why are we wasting the best of our youth on this needless war? Why are these boys blindly rushing into suicide at the whims of greedy, egotistical, self-motivated politicians and generals on both sides.

Heinrich begged his friend for an answer as if he actually expected one, "You are with God now so you must have all the answers. Tell me what either side has to gain that could make it worth this slaughter. The victor will not attain fortune, gold, land or any other tangible prize. I have never heard of combatants and enemies sacrificing so much with so little to gain and no tangible cause for war.

"The world can call me a coward if they must, but to me it is not a coward who would stand before the leaders of this nation and say, 'This is a needless war of greed and self-gratification.'"

Then Heinrich spotted a letter that Fish had crudely written and tucked inside his sackcoat:

"People think they understand, but they really have no clue of the life of a soldier and what it is we have to go through, fighting for those who cannot, and for those who burn what we swore to defend...

"The soldier constantly experiences hunger, homesickness, anger, sadness, fear, thirst, exhaustion, loneliness and disgust. Sometimes I feel small, helpless and alone in a world hard of finding trust, with nothing to do but wait for another day.

"We are soldiers, men of honor, holding steadfast and strong, without fear, even though we will be haunted by the images left in our heads, and by the ghosts and nightmares...

"Even when the fighting is done you always wonder why you put yourself through it...Is it out of pure patriotism, fear or just to defend our nation's people?"

Heinrich began to wonder over his future and his place in the war. He was afraid that if he tried to go back to the 10th Ohio Cavalry, at this point, he might have a hard time explaining his absence, including the time in Libby Prison. If they don't believe his story they might accuse him of being a deserter and have him executed.

Ironically, for the first time since the war began more than two years ago, he found himself back in his home state of Pennsylvania. Here he was only a few days walk from Erie, yet, as he sat there surrounded by the bodies of many boys he grew up with, he knew there was only one of two ways he could ever return there again – a Civil War hero, or dead. If he returned before the end of the war he would be held in dishonor.

The emotions were running wild in the 21-year-old, who had already experienced so much pain and sacrifice in the past year and now found himself thrust in to a situation that he could not win, and, in all likelihood, would end in his death.

Strangely though, in the midst of all the horror, Heinrich felt a new, refreshingly optimistic emotion that he had never really experienced before – love. Through all the fright he was witnessing, Heinrich saw a sudden visage of Mary Miller. Even though he had only known her for a few days, he was able to easily recall the beautiful image and longed to be with her as soon as possible. At the same time, he became gripped with guilt while he stood there surrounded by bodies of young soldiers, many of whom he had grown up with, who would never again see their loved ones.

Heinrich was scared, alone and confused, but he knew he had to do something. He started by dragging Fish's body to a shady, secluded spot right there on the southern slope of Little Round Top. He grabbed a shovel and labored most of the afternoon digging shallow graves for many of the dead including the confederate, Sgt. Alexander Hensel.

He saved the most respectable gravesite he could for Fish. He figured eventually either family or volunteers would come and give him a proper burial in a cemetery. He took two pieces of wood to form a cross and crudely scrawled the words:

"Sgt. Duane B. Fish, 83rd Pa,. warrior of Little Round Top, died in the face of confederate fire July 2, 1863."

CHAPTER 9

HE NEEDS TO BE WITH MARY

einrich felt his mind going back to Mary and realized that he could not pass up the opportunity to at least see her one more time before deciding where to go from there. Slowly he trudged his way across the gruesome battlefield in search of where he and Mr. Miller had agreed to meet.

He found his friend assisting other volunteers with the dead and wounded.

"Mr. Miller did you find your son's body?" Heinrich asked.

"Not exactly," Miller responded. "They tell me that volunteers could not identify a lot of the boys. So they placed many of them in massive, common pits with other boys from their own states," Miller said, as he lowered his head and then slowly gazed to his right toward Cemetery Hill.

"They tell me he's in a grave full of unknown soldiers, Miller said, as tears flowed down his face.

"What is there stopping us from opening the grave and looking for his body," Heinrich asked.

"If he's up there with other boys from Troy, then he's among his friends and fellow union soldiers. I know that he would say there is no better place for him to spend eternity than here at Gettysburg," Miller said.

With that, the duo headed back to their wagon in search of Mary. Heinrich told her about Little Round Top then Miller explained about her brother.

"I can honestly admit now that I am afraid, but more than that, I am confused," Heinrich told her. "It is my duty to be involved in this war and if I could save this precious union by laying down my own life, I would gladly do so right now.

"But the needless waste of lives… for what purpose."

He continued, "Mary I know this is abrupt but I find myself strongly attracted to you and would be greatly honored if you would allow me to ride north with you while I attempt to sort through my thoughts," Heinrich said.

"I would love for you to accompany us, and perhaps I can help you in your decisions," the young maiden responded.

The trio steadily headed north, involved in very pleasant conversation. Heinrich and Mary bonded so naturally and quickly, it was as if they had known each other for ever, she said. For the first time in years, he was able to escape the civil war and put his mind and enthusiasm in to something else, even if it was only temporary.

Heinrich told Mary how he had run away as a young teenager and travelled with the Dan Rice's Circus as a tumbler. She told him how she was raised by her father because her mother "was not of the best reputation," in Troy. "My mother was not a good woman," she said.

Mary went on to tell Heinrich that her brother's name was Charles and that he was only a few years older than her. My parents were quite young when he was born and they were unmarried. My father did not know that she was even pregnant until he found the-new-born, Charles in a basket, on his doorstep, along with a crude note from our mother. The note said that she was not ready to be a wife or mother. My father was heart-broken because he loved her so and intended to ask her to marry him; instead he was left to raise an infant by himself.

By 1848 my mother showed up once-again at my father's doorstep pleading for him to take her back. He lovingly agreed in hopes that they would be married and the three of them could form a happy family, which was not to be the case.

"I was born in 1850," and was apparently too much of a burden to my mother because she left my father alone with us when I was an infant, never to return to our lives on a regular basis again. My father worked hard in the mills of Troy to support the three of us, while Charles attended school and helped my father raise me.

"He was more like a parent to me than a big brother. My father taught us all he could about life and the importance of being good, upstanding, loyal, citizens in this great country of America.

"That's why Charles did not hesitate in 1862 to join the union army and to do his part to preserve our great union against those cussed secessionists who have now claimed his valiant life," Mary said. Charles was not old enough to enlist at the time so father gave him the permission to lie about his age and even enter the army under an assumed name. I am not sure what that name might have been.

"Oh, how I cried when he enlisted because deep-down I knew I would never see him again. I would not let him see me cry because he was so proud and full of confidence. He told me not to cry over his enlisting, nor even if he were to be killed."

Mary said that the night before he left for war he wrote her this letter:

"Mary, our lives have been difficult ones. Our mother can not even prove our births, nor does she seem to care that we have existed for all of these years. But you, I, and father do care tremendously for each other, and we are all that each of us has.

"Mary, for this reason alone I must make this commitment to fight those who would rebel against our great land and endeavor to split it in two. It is my duty, if necessary, to lay down my life in its defense,

so you and father shall have a safe place to live and raise our future generations.

"Father and I have engaged in great debate, unbeknownst to you, because he felt it his duty to enlist in the union army. It was only after arduous words that I was finally able to convince him that being younger; I would be much more of an asset to the army than he. I was able to help him realize that you need him in your life much more than you need me.

"Do not cry if it is my destiny to shed this mortal burden for in its stead I shall proceed directly to the waiting arms of our maker where I will remain for eternity – a proud union soldier in service to his family, country and, most of all, God.

"Mary, if this be the case, then, inquire of my 'pards' from Troy – 'Did he die with his face toward the enemy?' If that is so, then know that I died proud while fighting the confederate army. Know that I never showed them my backside, or any indication of a white feather. Of this fact, you should celebrate and rather than shed a tear, speak with pride of the name, Pvt. Charles Miller.

"Mary it is my ultimate prayer that someday there shall be some curious, young, great-grandchild of yours who will question, 'Were any of my ancestors in the Civil War? Did he really fight off those confederates?'

- *Please show him this letter and let him know to continue our proud legacy!*
- *Signed with undying love and loyalty,*
- *Pvt. Charles J. Miller, soldier in service to the great Army of the Republic, the United States of America.*

Mary lowered her head as she conveyed the contents of the letter to Heinrich, then rapidly gazed up toward him with a bright smile. "I cried when I read the news of his death but I have not shed a tear since. His inspiration and optimism give me encouragement to keep his legacy alive and to lead my life in a fashion that would make my older brother proud.

In fact, "I've decided that my first born son shall have the name of Charles," Mary said.

Heinrich suddenly lunged forward about to verbalize – "Charles Thibaut, what a wonderful name," but realized his enthusiasm may frighten the youthful maiden.

The trio continued on their trip to Troy, New York as Heinrich struggled with his future. Each passing day seemed to make the decisions no clearer than the previous because all he could think about was his growing passion for Mary.

At one point they stopped near a river to bathe and refresh themselves. As Mary enjoyed her private time Heinrich made his away along the riverbed looking for interesting shells and stones.

As they proceeded on their wagon trip a short time later Mary curiously noticed Heinrich patiently grinding stones together and filing with a crude instrument.

A few hours later her fascination got the best of her. "Are you that frustrated that you need to vent by crushing rocks," she inquired.

Heinrich looked up and smiled at her as he reached the palm of his hand gently into hers. "I'm sorry Mary, did I neglect to tell you that I am a molder by trade. It has been a long time since I've been able to ply my craft," he responded.

Mary slowly turned her palm upward and spread her fingers to reveal a glistening ring and necklace featuring multiple shades and colors of gems, stones and shells. "Is it really mine? This is the grandest, most beautiful gift anyone has ever given me.

"I love it," she said, as tears of joy radiated down her smooth young face. Heinrich reached to gently wipe the tears with his hand as Mary swept into his arms with a loving embrace and a kiss.

"But I love you even more," she said. "I love you too," Heinrich rapidly responded.

CHAPTER 10

LIFE IN TROY, NEW YORK AFTER GETTYSBURG

H einrich and the Millers finally arrived in Troy during late July 1863. Mr. Miller helped Heinrich get a temporary job to support himself as a molder in a local mill that employed many of the increasing number of immigrants who came to this country during the mid-1800s. Germans and Irish represented the working-poor classes of citizens in Troy, as they did throughout most northern cities during those times.

Heinrich made quick friends in the mill and in the neighborhood including a gentleman named Louis Wink, with whom he boarded for a period.

Troy and surrounding cities, including Albany and Rensselaer were as affected by the Civil War as much as any other city in the north by 1863. The cities were basically drained of any military-aged men, many of whom were currently serving, or had already been counted among the casualties.

Troy felt the pain of Gettysburg particularly, because it was the first major engagement for the 125th New York Regimental Volunteers.

The 125th was organized in Troy and mustered into service for three years, beginning August 27, 1862. They left Troy four days later, headed for what they-hoped-to-be, the seat of war. On September 16 they had the misfortune of being only as far as Harper's Ferry, Va., when Conf. Gen. Stonewall Jackson and his troops surrounded the garrison and demanded its surrender, including all other federal troops in the area.

The 125th accidentally became part of the largest surrender of troops in United States history as approximately 12,500 men were turned over to the confederate army.

Jackson's capture of Harper's Ferry enabled Gen. Lee to make a stand at Sharpsburg, Maryland which led to the Battle of Antietam the following day – the bloodiest single day in United States history as more than 21,000 Americans from both sides became casualties.

The men of the 125th were eventually paroled and sent to Camp Douglas, Illinois for more than three months to await assignment.

Parole is the period term used when one side exchanges the enemy's prisoners of war for an equivalent number of their own. This was a common practice during the early years of the war but, after Gettysburg, Union Gen. Ulysses S. Grant decided to stop the program because he felt the union army could afford to have soldiers taken out of the action, while he hoped the impact would become harmful to the confederacy.

From there 125th members were garrisoned to forts around Washington, D.C., where they were rigorously trained. In June of 1863 they formed part of the new 3rd Brigade, 3rd Division, 2nd Army Corps., composed of the 39th, 111th and 126th New York Regiments. Their commander was the tough regular army officer Alexander Hayes. Col. George Lamb Willard, who had been with the 125th since it's inception, was made the 3rd Brigade Commander.

Within a month of formation the 125th, and the rest of the 3rd Brigade made their bloody debut at Gettysburg, where the 125th suffered 139 casualties, including-their-beloved Col. Willard.

The loss of Willard was considered avenged though as the 125th was credited with firing the round that claimed the life of Conf. Gen. Barksdale on July 2. On July 3rd they held the Bryan Farm area of the "stone wall," the objective of Pickett's Charge.

There were 139 men from the 125th New York Regimental Volunteers who were killed, wounded or missing at the Battle of Gettysburg from 500 who were engaged. Of the 867 New Yorkers buried at the national cemetery at Gettysburg, 11 of them were known members of the 125th.

The 125th would go on to suffer 136 casualties in Grant's "Overland Campaign" in the spring of 1864 and 20 more in the trenches of the long, dreary siege of Petersburg. At Weldon Railroad that same June the casualties numbered 85; while at Reams Station, the regiment lost 22.

At the end of March 1865, the regiment lost 32 men in the repulse of the final, desperate confederate attacks on the union trenches, and pursued Lee's Army to Appomattox. After marching in the Grand Review of the Army at Washington in May, the 125th finally returned to Troy, where the men received their final payment, and mustered out on June 15, 1865.

Ironically, Heinrich arrived in Troy from Gettysburg about the same time as Col. Willard's body and those of many members of area regiments, including 125th.

There was much pain and mourning throughout the city following the Battle of Gettysburg, which ultimately became the height and turning point of the war.

George Lamb Willard was born in New York City on Aug. 15, 1827. His direct lineage included soldiers of distinction in the Revolutionary War and the War of 1812. He first made a name for himself and rose to national acclaim as the first sergeant of his company while serving with the Fifteenth Ohio Volunteers during the Mexican War.

His commission as colonel of the 125th bears the date of Aug. 15, 1862. He immediately became admired by his men and residents of

Troy. But less than a year later his body would be sent back to Troy where he was deeply mourned. He was buried in Oakwood Cemetery, which is one of the largest cemeteries in Rensselaer County.

As much as Troy was gripped by battle losses during July 1863, another offshoot of the Civil War also had a deadly, chilling affect on that area. For the first time in American history, the military draft was instituted.

There were draft riots in New York City that spiraled to Troy and many other major cities in the north because it seemed to single out poor minorities and immigrants while offering exclusions to those with the money to finance their way around it.

The Union Conscription Act of Mar. 3, 1863, provided that all able-bodied males between the ages of 20 and 45 were liable to military service, but a drafted man who furnished an acceptable substitute or paid the government $300 was excused. This allowed the rich to buy their way out of the draft, but left the poor, mostly inner-city Irish and German immigrants, with no options. This led to the popular phrase of the time, "Rich man's war, but a poor man's fight," and ignited rioters to vent their frustration mostly on innocent Negroes. By this time in the war, many people began to believe the war was more about freeing slaves than saving the union.

The draft, widely considered a defective piece of legislation, and enforced amid great unpopularity, provoked nationwide disturbances that were most serious in New York City on July 13-16, 1863. There, large-scale, bloody riots occurred. Many elements in New York sympathized with the South, and the war had aggravated long-standing economic and social grievances. Aroused by the statements of Gov. Horatio Seymour and other Democratic leaders that the conscription act was unconstitutional, the populace was incited to action.

Laborers, mostly Irish-Americans, made up the bulk of a tremendous mob that overpowered police and militia, attacked and seized the Second Ave. armory containing rifles and guns, and set fire to many buildings. Abolitionists and blacks were especially singled out for attack. Many blacks were tortured and brutally beaten to death, and a black orphanage was burned, leaving hundreds of children homeless. Business ceased, while robbing and looting flourished.

Meanwhile, New York troops, including the famous 7th Regiment, which had been to the front for the Gettysburg campaign, only days prior, were rushed in. With the aid of the police, militia, naval forces, and cadets from West Point, they were able to restore order.

But in the end, the riots had inflicted property damage of $1.5 million to $ 2 million, and it has been estimated that total casualties ran as high as 1,000, including many rioters themselves as well as police officers, military, but mostly innocent civilians, especially Negroes.

On a lesser scale, riots would spread to many northern cities during that heated summer, including Troy, making Heinrich Thibaut's quandary even more difficult.

Many Irish immigrants arrived in Troy during the 1840s as a result of the great potato famine in their home country. These hard working people competed with other ethnic groups and natives to secure jobs in the rapidly growing collar, cuff, iron and domestic industries. As did other groups, they formed their own churches and neighborhoods.

Just as in New York City, the Irish and other poor, working-class minorities in that area felt they were being singled-out by the draft to carry on the Civil War fight. The blazing issue of abolishing slavery was at the forefront for starting the war, and, now for perpetuating it.

The mixed feelings that prevailed in Troy at the time both hurt, and helped Heinrich as he attempted to "blend in" and eek out a living for himself, while wrestling with where his place was in respect to the war. Also, causing mixed emotions for him was his love for Mary, which was growing stronger daily.

Southern sympathizers and so-called "Copperheads," (legislators and elected officials who promoted a negotiated peace that would result in southern independence) were prevalent in Troy, as in many other northern cities. They were intermingled with strong northern supporters who were still committed to fight to the death to save the union and free slaves in the process.

With the war more than two years old at that point, the idea of negotiating was out of the question for many because so much had been sacrificed in terms of resources and manpower. President Lincoln often mentioned that sentiment in his public speeches, while flatly refusing to even recognize the confederate government as an existing entity that he would have to negotiate with. Most northerners and southerners, alike, felt if they did not continue to "fight to the death" they would be letting down those who had already met demise on the battlefield.

Because he was a stranger in a new city Heinrich did not feel immediate personal pressure to enlist in the union army, but as he got to know more people, they began to question him.

He turned 22 years old during October 1863 in a city that had already sacrificed many of its brothers, fathers, and cousins and loved ones in the war, yet here he stood as an apparent civilian. Heinrich explained to some of his closer associates how he had enlisted with the 10th Ohio Calvary, escaped from Libby Prison and made his way around the confederate army. He was also still very handicapped by his two serious wounds. Even though they weren't actual battle wounds, Heinrich explained how he had been struck on right side of his neck by a saber during a raid and shot in the right shoulder by a rebel picket just before he met the escaped slave, Josef. These still tormented him and left him very awkward and limited on his right side and left him to wonder whether he would be able to perform the duties of a union private.

Through it all though there was a certain amount of pressure on Heinrich, both from others and himself, to rejoin the union army. But as weeks became months he grew closer to Mary and struggled to eek out a living for himself in hopes of someday asking Mary to become his wife, but he new he could not accomplish that while the war was still raging. The one very slim hope that he clung to during this period was that the war would come to an end during 1863.

Heinrich once told an acquaintance in Troy, "This war has gone on long enough. There has been plenty of death, sacrifice and destruction to satisfy even the harshest war monger. I think any reasonable man can plainly see it's time to end it either through negotiation or some form of communication."

But now Heinrich found himself in an unfamiliar city having journeyed through so much and so seen much in less than a full year in the union army.

The Battle of Gettysburg did turn the tide of the war in favor of the union for the first time. Prior to that, confederate victories at places such Bull Run, Fredericksburg and Chancellorsville had not only given the south the feeling that its army was invincible, but also that they could win the war and gain their independence. The victory at Gettysburg was followed by a major boost for the federals on July 4, 1863 when the City of Vicksburg finally surrendered to Grant after months of non-stop siege and bombardment.

CHAPTER 11

THE WAR RAGES ON

A s Heinrich remained in Troy and Gen. Meade's Army of the Potomac went into winter camp during late 1863-64, the war continued to rage on other fronts. On the Western Theater of Operations on Sept. 19-20 Maj. Gen. William S. Rosencrans and Gen. Braxton Bragg finally squared off against each other at Chickamauga Creek, just south of Chattanooga, Tennessee. Bragg won a great victory but then frittered away the advantage when he declined to pursue the beaten Union forces, to the intense disgust of Cavalry Gen. Nathan Bedford Forrest, who had been sorely harassing them. Despite the shattering defeat Union Gen. George Thomas gained the sobriquet "The Rock of Chickamauga" for holding his ground while others fled and then making a safe orderly withdrawal toward Chattanooga.

Two months later on Nov. 24-25, Gen. Grant would get even with Bragg and put an end to his field command at the Battle of Chattanooga when his Army of the Cumberland, with some units from the Army of the Potomac, gained an overwhelming victory from what seemed an impossible situation. Gen. Joseph "Fighting Joe" Hooker's, union men attacked up the rugged Lookout Mountain and gradually encircled the base of the mountain. The heavily out-numbered, and badly-beaten defenders could do little but hold out until night covered their withdrawl to nearby Missionary Ridge. The

Confederate Army went from a position of overwhelming advantage high on the mountain to a humiliating defeat.

Lee and Grant met directly in battle on May 5-6, 1864 at an area known as the Wilderness, located 14 miles west of Fredericksburg. The Army of the Potomac met squarely with the Army of Northern Virginia for the first time in months as the battle that ended in a draw proved nothing more than there was to be no quick end to the war. However, unlike his predecessors, Grant proved he would not give up on his task of winning the war and destroying Lee's army in the process.

The two generals would meet days later at the battle of Spotsylvania which raged from May 8-18 and took place 12 miles southwest of Fredericksburg. The vicious battle that evolved into ferocious hand-to-hand combat at "Bloody Angle" proved once again that Grant would not allow his army to be beaten and that it was south of the Rapidan and would stay there if it "takes all summer."

It finally did become early summer 1864 and Heinrich had struggled with choices while trying to maintain his relationship with Mary. He had previously reasoned that the best and the only place for him, was as a soldier in the union army, despite any personal feelings he may have about the war. "I made the commitment at the outset of the war and my feelings have not changed. My country needs me more now than ever, even if it means sacrificing my life in its defense." He struggled with how he was going to tell Mary of his decision, and ask her to wait for his return.

One time after a heavy night of alcohol consumption with a few of his buddies, Heinrich decided to pay Mary a visit.

Mary met him and invited him to sit on couch beside her. In a short period they began to embrace romantically and became more passionate. Suddenly, Mary's father entered the home a found them in the heat of passion.

Without saying a word, Mr. Miller went over to Heinrich, grabbed him by the collar and the seat of his pants and hurled him directly through the picture window of the family home directly in to the street. Mary started to run to his aid when her father grasped her firmly by the wrist and said, "No. If he really loves you he'll come back in here and face me again."

There, Heinrich laid all night in a drunken stuper covered in his own blood and vomit wondering if this is really what his life has been reduced to.

As morning finally arrived Heinrich picked himself up, shortly after Mr. Miller left for work, and went to directly to a glazer where he purchased the correct size glass. He spent much of the day replacing the window and then waited outside for the old man to return.

"May I come in?" Heinrich requested, as Miller approached him. Miller glanced at the new window and nodded approvingly toward the door. Mary eagerly met the two men in the parlor and ran to embrace Heinrich.

"I am glad you came back in without hesitation, Heinrich. If you hadn't, you would have lost my respect completely. You've shown that you have some courage, but there's more you need to prove before you can have my daughter's hand in marriage."

Heinrich knew where he was going with the conversation and lunged eagerly to tell Mr. Miller and Mary that he was about to enlist in a Troy regiment, but before he could get all the words out, Miller raised his hand to silence him.

"I have just lost my only son to this war. I will not let him die in vain. I would much rather have my daughter wandering the streets of Troy mourning your death as a soldier, than to stroll those streets on the arm of a coward," he said to Heinrich.

CHAPTER 12

ENLISTS IN THE 91ST NEW YORK

On Aug. 31 1864 Heinrich Thibaut enlisted for one year in the 91st New York Regimental Infantry in Albany under the assumed name of Henry Lyons (his buddy who was killed in the raid.) He was paid a bounty of $33.33 and took that name after his old buddy because he was concerned that if he went in under his own name the connection would be made from the 10th Ohio and he would be accused of being a deserter or bounty jumper.

The 91st had already established a proud fighting reputation as a veteran regiment that was organized and mustered into United States service on Dec 16, 1861 at the Industrial School barracks on the New Scotland plank road in Albany with Jacob Van Zandt and Jonathan Tarbell as their colonel and lieutenant colonel, respectively.

They were sent first to Key West, Fla. And became part of the garrison in Pensacola where they saw their first action in raids into north Florida and south Alabama. In 1863 the 91st became part of General Bank's command (XIX Corps) and fought at Irish Bend, Vermillion Bayou and Port Hudson in Louisiana.

During the winter of 1863/64 they were sent to Fort Jackson to be paid and mustered for re-enlistment but ended up detained for most of the winter where many men became ill. By the summer there was scarcely a healthy man in the regiment.

The regiment arrived in Albany on July 19, 1864 on a thirty day furlough to an enthusiastic welcome. They began a recruiting effort which helped lead to Heinrich enlisting.

By 1864 they had earned the recognition of being a veteran regiment, since they had seen so much action. Heinrich was among those new recruits to reinforce them. They were re-assigned to the Fifth Corps (the main fighting body of the Union Army by then) which would ultimately give Heinrich his first actual battle exposure at White Oak Road and Five Forks, Va., in pursuit of Lee's Army of Northern Virginia in the Appomattox Campaign during the spring of 1865.

But, before Heinrich could get on with his military life and fulfill the obligation he'd volunteered for more than three years prior, he had to set his personal feelings, and beliefs aside. This included saying a tearful, emotional goodbye to Mary with a promise that he would return to Troy after the war.

By Sept. 13, 1864 the 91st New York Regimental Volunteers were stationed at Hart Island, NY, listed as a veteran regiment, with Heinrich Thibaut present and finally back in full military uniform

By the end of September the regiment was stationed at Ft. McHenry, Maryland, where they would remain in winter camp until needed on the front with the Army of the Potomac in February.

By winter the union and confederate armies had spent the previous three-and-half years engaged in regular bloody combat to determine whether the southern states could secede from the United States and actually form a new country and government. Yet, they remained at a standoff with neither side really being able to deliver the crushing blow it would take to win the war and finally end it.

President Abraham Lincoln was not happy with the way the war had been dragging on. Yes, there had been some recent victories and the north was becoming more confident that there would be an eventual victory for them, but something had to be done to quicken that pace.

In March of 1864, Lincoln had appointed Ulysses S. Grant, lieutenant general, the highest ranking position in the U.S. Army. Months later Lincoln and his new general turned to Grant's old friend and his successor in the West, Maj. Gen. William Tecumseh Sherman. Together they plotted their spring offensive. At the heart of that offense was the intention to use the vast resources and manpower of the federal side to place pressure on the confederate army and its government on all fronts until they cracked.

The plan evolved that Sherman would aim his veteran, and previously very successful army, directly at Atlanta, with the objective, as Grant would later write, "…to break it up and get into the interior of the enemy's country as far as you can, inflicting all the damage you can against their war resources."

As Sherman waged war on the material resources of Dixie, Grant planned to surround Gen. Lee's rebel army in Virginia and break through to make his way to the confederate capital in Richmond.

By the fall of 1864 Sherman had battled his way into undisputed possession of Atlanta, which he proceeded to virtually destroy. On November 16, 1864, Sherman marched out of Atlanta with nearly the entire city ablaze and advanced his 60,000 veteran troops southeast, deep into Georgia. He directed them to move rapidly and live off the land while destroying anything of military value between Atlanta and Savannah. The risks of his now-famous, "March to the Sea," would be great but the rewards would be greater he told them.

Sherman's successful campaign would cut the confederacy in two, north and south, and allow him to come at Lee's Army of Northern Virginia from the south as Grant continued to bear down on it from the north.

Sherman and his army cut a broad, burned swath of destruction and misery until his arrival in the port city of Savannah on December 22, 1864. The city surrendered without a fight, and, that same evening, the general sent a telegram to Lincoln, "I beg to present you as a Christmas gift the city of Savannah, with one hundred and fifty heavy guns and plenty of ammunition; also about twenty five bales of cotton."

But Sherman didn't stop there. He tore through South Carolina and then headed into North Carolina. He entered South Carolina because that is where the rebellion was born, he claimed. On February 16, 1865 Sherman's army reached the South Carolina capital of Columbia, leaving that city almost completely destroyed by fire. On February 18, confederate troops abandoned Ft. Sumter as Sherman closed in on Charleston. That city saw no point in making a stand since the rest of South Carolina had been reduced to a hollow shell. Charleston surrendered and the Stars and Stripes flew above Ft. Sumter for the first time since April 13, 1861.

CHAPTER 13

JOSEF AND HIS OFFSPRING UNITED

A major offshoot of Sherman's march was that many slaves believed the union army was there to free them so they abandoned the plantations and their masters in hordes. Many followed, praising "Uncle Billy" as their savior who was going to lead them to freedom. This led to what Heinrich would later say was his most satisfying moment of the entire war.

During early February he requested a few days furlough so he could leave Fort McHenry long enough to visit Amelia since she lived nearby. As he approached her house he could hear joy and music combined with loud excitement. He lightly knocked on her door which was promptly answered by the young negroe boy, Cylus. The boy motioned for Heinrich to enter the home. There he saw Amelia, Josef and many other negroes happily surrounding a young woman, who politely sat and smiled while answering their many questions. Suddenly, Josef came running over to Heinrich and joyfully hugged him.

"Come over Heinrich, your timing is perfect. Here's somebody I would like you to meet. This is my daughter LuLu...God has answered our prayers."

LuLu explained to Heinrich and the rest of the crowd how she realized when General Sherman and his troops came through the South Carolina plantation where she was a slave, that this was her one chance to escape and follow the underground railroad to her father.

"Before I left I walked directly to the mistress and informed her that I was finally setting myself free and that I was no longer under any obligation to her. I told her I was going to the plantation nearby and taking my son to freedom with me.

"I told her, "You know how you always told us that the Yankees are one-eyed monsters who would burn us alive and eat us. Well, now I know why you told us such a horrible exaggerated lie. General William T. Sherman came up to our house directly and informed us how he and his troops were our friends and they were setting us free to make our own way in this country.

"She cried and pleaded with me to stay and help her protect the plantation and her family since her husband is off to the war. She even promised to promote me to a position inside the house, but I promptly told her, "The days of the "house nigger" are also over, forever.

"Then I asked how she could possibly have the nerve to ask me to protect her children when she had sold mine."

LuLu went on to explain she gave birth to a son, but the mistress sold the boy to a neighboring plantation when he was about five years old. At that point, a bright young child about seven years old presented himself to Heinrich and reached out a dark, shiny, perfectly clean hand to shake, "How do you do, sir? My new full name is Joseph William Sherman."

Before my mother took me to freedom my name was only Joseph but since we have to make our way in this free land now, we all agreed to take the full surname of the man who freed us. Josef and LuLu walked over and hugged the boy.

"I didn't even know I had a grandson," Josef said. "Now I have my LuLu back and a child who bears my name and the name of a great man. It's funny because we were all born as slaves, but now, someday when the good lord comes for us, we will go to him as free people. *"Praise the Lord and Mssrs Lincoln, Sherman and Grant too."*

Heinrich asked if they were going to remain in Maryland or head further north.

"Oh, no we're headed back to South Carolina," Josef said. To which Heinrich responded with shock and surprise. "Why would you go back to a state that enslaved you and caused this horrible war?"

LuLu explained that when she was sold to the plantation as a young girl, the owner's daughter took a liking to her. "She took an enormous chance by teaching me to read and write. It was against the law in the south to educate a slave, but this child risked severe punishment for me."

There is word among the freed slaves that there is a plan to set up a negroe community on an island off the coast of South Carolina with the main purpose being to educate young negroe children. "I will go there to be a teacher," LuLu said. "I feel I owe this to society and it is my life's calling."

Heinrich spent the remainder of his furlough with the happy group, before bidding them a joyous farewell. "Da Lord is gonna end this cruel war very soon," Amelia told him as he left, and we will all be happy, safe and free forever, she said.

CHAPTER 14

ARMY LIFE

Heinrich's first six months – September 1864 to February 1865- included very little actual military action instead he had an extended stay in a hospital with a heavy cold, followed by influenza and then measles. He wrote to Mary that his bed was "fairly comfortable, but we have toast to eat, sometimes with butter and sometimes, even some meat." He said in some cases the measles had become fatal to some soldiers, but he told Mary not to worry about him as he was "feeling very strong at this time."

He talked about being very lonely at Fort McHenry despite the fact that he considered it a "splendid place." There were about three thousand troops garrisoned at the fort for the winter including about 700 with the 91st Regiment.

He sent Mary a letter talking about having to pay as much as $2.00 for a watermelon and about how there were more negroes in and around the fort than he had ever seen in one place. He said the food in the barracks was good, often consisting of fresh beef, pork and vegetables. The staples included beans, coffee and hardtack. Most of his day consisted of drilling. He also talked about how a deserter was executed at one point.

Heinrich also had strong political concerns during the fall of 1864 as Gen. George McClellan challenged Lincoln for the presidency. "Abe must be elected," Heinrich wrote to Mary, "The union will be preserved and the war will be brought to a speedy ending," he predicted. The feeling in the south was that "Little Mac" might be more willing to negotiate with them on a compromised peace, whereas, Lincoln proved he was willing to see the war played out rather than negotiate with an entity - the confederate government - which he refused to admit even existed.

His time at Ft. McHenry also presented Heinrich an opportunity to finally communicate with his family back in Erie. He wrote them of all of his experiences since joining the army, but his letters also consisted of numerous requests for items of basic comfort such as blankets, tooth brushes, paper for writing letters and food items, including cakes. He told them how those items were often stolen by other soldiers.

Finally, on February 22, 1865 the 91st Regiment was ordered to the front at Petersburg. They packed immediately and prepared to move out the next day. Heinrich wrote to Mary that emotions varied among the men about the news of potentially going to battle. Most were excited while some were "about half-scared to death." He said he was just happy to finally be leaving the garrison.

In March, Heinrich's company was ordered south to a camp near Hatcher's Run, a creek near Petersburg, Va., where they became embattled in the great siege. Heinrich talked of using large logs to construct living quarters as well as defensive positions, and of the possibility of being pounced on by rebels at any moment. We don't know what day or time we will be engaged and sent to battle the confederate army, he said. Since it is spring and Gen. Sheridan is about six miles away from us, driving the enemy in our direction, it will only be a matter of a few weeks, he predicted. By late March there were numerous skirmishes and occasional firing back-and-forth as the two sides closed near each other. There were also rumors that the long siege was nearing an end as Petersburg was inevitably going to fall into union hands.

CHAPTER 15

THE BATTLE OF FIVE FORKS

Within days, Heinrich's first exposure to warfare arrived when the union's 5th Corps, including the 91st, left camp for a 30-mile march that included some skirmishing and firing at nearly every juncture. "Now I am getting to know what real soldiering is like," Heinrich wrote to Mary, "I have finally fired my weapon at the enemy and have gone three days in a row without rations since we are on the march at all times." The regiment was even under fire at night so they all remained on alert with little time for sleep. The object of the 5th corps was to continue pressing Gen. Lee until they could bottle him up and surround him. Eventually, the retreating general would have no choice but to surrender his army or allow them to be destroyed, or taken as prisoners.

Grant's hope at Five Forks, Va., was to force Lee's army to abandon their fortifications guarding the approaches to Petersburg and destroy his army in the process.

The mood was so optimistic that on March 27, President Abraham Lincoln and his twelve-year-old son, reviewed the troops, including the 91st. The entourage also included the president's cabinet members and Gen. Grant with his staff. There were about 1800 soldiers from the 91st present that day, including Heinrich. The regiment was very proud to boast of their combat reputation to the dignitaries. Heinrich reported that he had recovered from his illnesses and was prepared for battle and enjoying being a soldier more everyday.

Major General Samuel Crawford was commander over the third division of the union's V Corps, which included the 91st. His officers were admonished to ensure that every man remained in the ranks and did not straggle. Major General Gouverneur K. Warren, V Corps commander, warned that, "any man may be justifiably shot who… (falls out) without permission from the division commander."

Near Hatcher's Run Petersburg, Va., on March 25, 1865 the men spent most of the day fighting. They took about 4,000 prisoners. They left for battle in the morning and all returned back to camp safely at night. Since there was continuous firing between the sides all night, the men of the 91st were packed and prepared to be called into battle at any moment.

When they were brought in to action at the battle of White Oak Road on March 31, the 91st immediately began to rake the rebel line with well-directed volleys causing a number of grayclads to veer off.

The 91st was assigned to the Fifth Army Corps under Major General Gouverneur K. Warren and Bvt. Major General Charles Griffen. Their Third Division commander was Bvt. Major General Samuel W. Crawford and the First Brigade commander was Colonel John A. Kellogg. The commander of the 91st was Colonel Jonathan Tarbell, who was wounded at the Battle of White Oak Road, and the 91st was left behind when Kellogg's brigade was ordered to retreat because the rebels had turned his flanks.

The men of the 91st had to conduct a fighting withdrawal and cut their way through several Confederate roadblocks. A number of minutes had elapsed before Tarbell had realized that his regiment was terribly alone. Rather than surrender, the colonel decided to fight his way out of the trap. The regiment fell back to the Holliday cabin where Tarbell succeeded in forming part of his regiment on the colors. He then decided to make one more unsuccessful stand against the charging confederate troops before beating a retreat.

In his "After Action Report," Col. Kellogg proudly proclaimed that his "command were the last organized troops to leave the field." Fighting would continue virtually non-stop for days as both sides made their way toward Five Forks, where, if the federals were able to be victorious, they would reach the Southside Railroad and cut the wagon roads leading to the west along the south bank of the Appomattox and all would be lost finally for the confederacy. Simply, the rebels had to defend their weak hold on Five Forks or it would be their final stand.

The men lay each night under heavy fire with their muskets in their hands and even veterans said they had never seen a campaign such as this. They were twice without rations for three days at a time and moving continuously. The idea was to keep Gen. Lee retreating until the union army could completely surround him and force surrender.

On March 31 the 91st was engaged in fighting from mid-afternoon until dark with the heaviest action coming the following day at Five Forks. By dawn on the morning of April 1, the men of the Fifth Corps were strangely happy just to be alive following the onslaught that spread death throughout the night.

The regiment was at the front of the fire most of the day on April 1 and suffered about ten casualties. They were involved in the heaviest fighting from about 11 a.m. until sundown. Heinrich said shot and shell were flying fast and hard. He was struck once in the arm but the bullet only glanced off his sleeve and left a good bruise. Another minie ball wizzed within inches of his face and slammed into a tree. Heinrich took a second to take out his knife and pry it out as a keepsake. At one point, they were forced to retreat across a brook with their knapsacks and contents heavily weighted by water. The rebels were charging at them through the woods. The regiment retreated to a point in the woods and then fought for an hour finally forcing the enemy to retreat. In all, the regiment had to fall back three times but the last time they were able to march right over the enemy works.

The fighting was as intense as any other battle of the war, as both sides pushed each other back and forth. Fighting often became hand-to-hand and bodies from both sides lay scattered all over the wooded terrain, according to accounts.

According to many witnesses, some of the confederates took off their hats and threw their guns on the ground. They cried and moaned for mercy but the Yanks showed them none. We did have to bat some of them over the head with the guns to get them out of the way.

Col. John A. Kellogg's brigade consisting of the 6th and 7th Wisconsin and the 91st New York suffered a combined 108 casualties during the three days of fighting.

At about 10 a.m. on Saturday April 1, Gen. Philip Sheridan received a message from Grant that he (Sheridan) has complete freedom of action. As the afternoon progressed Sheridan became increasingly anxious with the lack of infantry movement as his cavalry was forced to dismount in order to fight and were quickly running low on ammunition.

"This battle must be fought and won before sundown," he said.

Sheridan and his cavalry proved to be the heroes of the day. Armed with their breechloaders and either sharps single-shot carbines or Spencer seven-shot repeaters, they demoralized the confederates with their sheer volume of fire. Sheridan victoriously leaped with his horse over the earthworks in the midst of confederate prisoners. By the next day Confederate Gen. A.P. Hill was dead and the confederates finally abandoned Petersburg.

The battle of Five Forks marked the beginning of the end for the Army of Northern Virginia. Grant succeeded in crushing Lee's right flank and rendered untenable his position at Petersburg which the confederacy had held onto since the previous June. Lee then had to evacuate the Petersburg-Richmond area and move into the field without the protection of the earthworks.

The victory at Five Forks crushed the rebel's stronghold in Virginia and sealed their fate.

The union army now had uncontested access to the long-sought-after confederate capital of Richmond. By April 4 Pres. Lincoln freely wandered the streets of Richmond and sat in the Confederate Capitol Building while rebel Pres. Jefferson Davis was fleeing for his life into the deep south.

Lee was left to begin his slow retreat and ultimate surrender at Appomattox. Following the fall of Petersburg Lee took his Confederate Army of Northern Virginia, by then reduced to 35,000 starving men, fled Petersburg and Richmond and headed west. Lee was aiming at Amelia Court House, where he hoped to find a shipment of food and to place his army on the Danville Railroad for South Carolina. There he planned to join Gen. Joseph E. Johnston and continue the fight for the Confederacy. Meanwhile, realizing the fight was lost; rebel soldiers were deserting in droves.

CHAPTER 16

PEACE AT LAST

Grant knew he had to cut Lee off before he had a chance to join Johnston. He had Sheridan destroy the rails of the railroad on April 5. By April 7 Grant had Lee right where he wanted him and was confident enough to send a surrender demand under the flag of truce. Lee inquired about terms, but was still not ready to surrender. His army kept marching, but was steadily dissolving as it progressed. Finally, on April 9, they arrived at the town of Appomattox Court House, where they would find federal cavalry and infantry. Following a brief engagement a confederate staff member suggested to Lee that he order his remaining troops to disperse into the hills and continue an infinite guerilla campaign. Lee declined, saying the guerillas would become mere bands of marauders, and that rounding them up might be devastating to Virginia.

"There is nothing left for me to do but go and see General Grant and I would rather die a thousand deaths." Lee exclaimed.

The men agreed to meet in the parlor of the brick home belonging to Wilmer McLean. Ironically, McLean had earlier given up a house that had been shelled during the First Bull Run and had to come to Appomattox to escape the war, only to have it end in his parlor.

At the formal surrender ceremony on April 12, a fellow soldier in the 91st with Heinrich later wrote: "...we were on a hill and could see Lee and his whole Army. Lee and Grant met each other half way, Lee with a flag of truce. Grant took his word and marched the whole army in our lines at four o'clock. They fired salute all round us, the bands played and men cheered and had a big time. We have been lying with our pieces in the same place."

Heinrich said it was with mixed emotions that he watched those poor, yet-still-so-proud and brave rebel soldiers humbled as all watched their sacred flag taken down. He said many cried, including him, yet no-one jeered or jested. It was such a feeling of elation to witness the star spangled red, white and blue that has once again united our country, remain steadfast as the only colors silhouetted proudly beneath the early-April skies.

Although, frozen with interest and elated with the war's end and glorious victory, the hard sojourn into history at Appomattox Court House, still came at a difficult price for Heinrich. He wondered if Mary, and his family and friends back in Erie would judge him – as one who fled, or as one who had the courage to stand alone and ask – WHY?

The surrender effectively ended the Civil War as the north exploded in celebrations and the south was humbled. President Lincoln immediately began making plans for reconstruction of the south, completely unaware that plans were simultaneously being hatched to end his life within a few days.

CHAPTER 17

LINCOLN ASSASSINATION

The Fifth Corps slowly made its way from lower Virginia headed toward Washington when this crippling message was delivered on April 15:

"The President died this morning. Wilkes Booth the assassin. Secretary Seward dangerously wounded. The rest of the Cabinet, General Grant, and other high officers of the Government Included in the plot of destruction."

Heinrich was paralyzed with emotion, as was the rest of the country, including the South when word of Lincoln's death reached the troops. The soldiers were so overcome they spoke of brutal vengeance including hypothetical attacks on rebel leaders such as Jefferson Davis. Treachery had infected the government and no-one knew how deep it ran at the time. Rumors were rampant; including strong fears of a confederate plot which could thrust the entire country back in to war.

A double guard was placed on the entire camp and leave was cancelled. Heinrich possessed an enormous admiration for Lincoln and recalled the sadness he had seen on that honest, yet tired, old face, only a few weeks prior. Heinrich had commented to a fellow soldier at the time that Lincoln's face showed much torture and personal stress as a result of the formidable task of trying to rescue the country from the rebels.

Union leaders seemed to believe that there was a plot to wreak havoc on the government in Washington because the confederacy still had the means and motivation to rush on the capital city. They concluded their only defense was to race to Washington before them and place Grant as a military dictator until a more constitutional government could be restored. But, this idea was scrapped until early May when the Army of The Potomac was ordered to start for Richmond.

Emotion once again gripped Heinrich as the first place the Fifth Corps passed on its way north was the battlefield at Five Forks where many comrades laid down their lives followed by the exact spot where Lincoln stood when Heinrich first laid eyes on him. Heinrich was also reminded of the horror of the aftermath of battle again one night when he was gathering firewood. He suddenly plunged in to a soft spot in the ground and quickly recovered to discover he had stumbled into a decaying body buried under some leaves and a thin layer of dirt. To make the horrific experience even worse he realized that in the darkness there were many ghastly bodies in similar condition. Many sculls and human bones were strewn as if part of some demonic festival. This brought back memories of Gettysburg to him.

From Five Forks Heinrich was next amazed at the abandoned former confederate capitol of Richmond. After four long years of constantly hearing how the union army must "March onto Richmond," and make that city their own, it was so rewarding for them to finally achieve that.

From there it was on to the nation's capital of Washington on the morning of May 23, 1865 for the final grand review of the

Army, which extended from the Capitol to the White House along Pennsylvania Avenue. Heinrich was proud and excited to parade with the victorious Army of the Potomac in front of all the dignitaries and military leaders, including the new President of the United States Andrew Johnson. But, at the same time he felt a little out of place because he was surrounded by real heroes who had fought, suffered and saw their comrades die on the countless battlefields of the past four years. His war was fought in a different vein. Yet, still the dream of final victory was so great and rewarding for everyone. At last, there was one final march and then tearful good-byes.

For Heinrich, the war finally came to a personal end on June 10, 1865 when he was given his second installment of $33.33 and an honorable discharge under the name of Henry Lyons. The discharge was from the 91st New York and given to him and fellow soldiers near Mount Washington while regimental bands played Auld Lang Syne and Home Sweet Home. The emotion and those songs made him long for Mary more than ever. For the first time in more than four years he was now completely free to tread in any direction he chose. His choice was to rush to his waiting love in Troy with a plan to eventually contact his family in Erie.

CHAPTER 18

A PEACEFUL LIFE AT LAST

The couple was finally united and went on to have five children, while Heinrich provided for them by working as a molder in various mills.

The industrial revolution followed on the heels of the Civil War leading to wealth, opportunity, growth and opulence throughout the country that was unheard of before 1861. Northern industry flourished with the sudden influx of cheap immigrant labor pouring in from all parts of the globe. Cities swelled, the railroad spread across the country and the unexplored west slowly became the tamed west. Many Civil War veterans and their children jumped on the opportunities for wealth, with the offspring carrying the lessons of the terrible war into the new century. The nation rose as a single beacon to the rest of the world as a land of freedom and unlimited opportunity.

Many claimed the war could have easily been avoided through negotiation and that the causes of the war would have eventually dissolved and narrowed the gap between the two parts of the country. The common feeling on both sides was that slavery would have eventually phased itself out naturally by the arrival of the new century.

Heinrich barely ever referred to the war, preferring to bury the memories but clinging to its lessons. He told Mary and his children of being held in the confederate prison and escaping, but offered little detail of battle.

He died of a pulmonary aneurism at the age of 45 in 1886 leaving behind a young destitute family. They resided in Erie for a few years, which is where he died. Mary gathered her courage and her brood and moved back to Troy, where she struggled to support them by taking in boarders and doing laundry for area residents. She collected a monthly military widow's pension of less than $10.

Heinrich's grave would go virtually ignored for nearly 116 years until 2002 when this writer would get down on his hands and knees to scrape debris, dirt and vegetation that covered the majority of a small stone that laid flat against the ground.

My efforts would be immediately rewarded though when, I had one of the biggest thrills of my life – his stone reads "91st NY Reg. Vols."

AFTERWORD

This book is based on the life of an actual Civil War soldier named Henry Dippo. He grew up in Erie, Pa. and had five children with Mary Miller, of Troy, N.Y, following the Civil War.

He is my great-great grandfather.

The Civil War has been one of my lifetime passions. It began as a toddler while getting "horsey rides" on my father's knee during the early 1950s.

Him and I would watch countless "cowboy" shows and movies and talk about the heroes and their accomplishments, including names of our great American actors such as John Wayne, Roy Rogers and Gary Cooper.

My father told me that someday him and I would go out west and become cowboys and Civil War soldiers.

I knew about the Civil War long before entering kindergarten, which means probably before I could read or write. That also means before I discovered other things such as baseball, fast cars and girls.

I remember by third grade I had exhausted my school library of Civil War books about the heroes, battles and generals. I grabbed any book even remotely associated with the war including biographies of George Washington Carver and Clara Barton.

Carver was a former slave, who was an inventor, chemist, botanist, scientist, and teacher. Carver is best known for the many uses he devised for the peanut.

Barton was known as "The Angel of the battlefield," by Civil War soldiers because of her voluntary nursing and life-saving skills. She was the founder of the American Red Cross after the war.

When I was about 10 ten years old in 1961, one Saturday afternoon I asked my grandmother, Dorothy (Connell/Spotten,) maiden name Dippo, if any of her ancestors were in the Civil War. She said, she thought that her grandfather was and her brother would have information about him to share with me.

She went on to say one of the most exciting things I had ever heard in my life.

"He might even have his pistol and if he does I'll ask him to give it to you," she said, then she added that we would go see him next Saturday afternoon. It still remains the longest week of my life.

I couldn't focus on anything else, especially school. I stared at the clock and counted the minutes.

Finally, the day came, and for the first time I met my father's Uncle, Ellsworth "ICHY" Dippo, who was about 60 years old at the time. I stood there sweating and shaking as he told me the story that he grew up with, and the only thing he knew, was that Henry Dippo was a Union soldier who had escaped from a confederate prison camp.

I wanted so desperately for him to tell me that he was a hero of such battles with names like Gettysburg, Shiloh and Antietam, and then present me with his pistol and maybe even a hat or a uniform, but he didn't.

Finally, I got up the nerve and said, my grandmother said you still have his pistol and you might give it to me.

"Oh, I had it for a long time. It laid around collecting dust so I sold it to a guy here in Troy, way back when, for a beer and a few dollars so he could hang it up in his bar."

Fifty Three years later, I still feel the painful agony of that moment that will forever be frozen in time for me the same as the John F. Kennedy assassination and the horrors of September 11, 2001.

In writing this novel, following a lifetime of research, I tried to make Henry Dippo a bonafide Civil War hero, which he was not. But, instead, I placed myself into what I thought his feelings, values, thoughts and emotions would have been during this horrific crisis, hence a well-embellished novel.

He is buried in Erie Cemetery, Erie, Pa., and his stone does read "91st NY Reg. Vols." He was present for duty on April 1, 1865 during the Battle of Five Forks in Virginia.

After his death, Mary (Miller) Dippo did leave Erie and returned to her hometown of Troy, N.Y., where she raised her children including my great-grandfather, Charles Dippo.

"IS POPS A VETERAN?"
"YES HE IS."
"DID HE FIGHT IN A WAR?"
"NO, BUT HE DID WRITE A BOOK!"